FANTASTICS AND OTHER FANCIES

FANTASTICS
AND OTHER FANCIES

BY

LAFCADIO HEARN

EDITED BY

CHARLES WOODWARD HUTSON

WILDSIDE PRESS
BERKELEY HEIGHTS · NEW JERSEY

Another great publication from...

Wildside Press
PO Box 45
Gillette, NJ 07933-0045
www.wildsidepress.com

First Wildside Press edition:
September 2000

There are tropical lilies which are venomous,
but they are more beautiful than the frail
and icy-white lilies of the North.

Lafcadio Hearn.

CONTENTS

CONTENTS

CONTENTS

CONTENTS

INTRODUCTION

INTRODUCTION

"I AM conscious they are only trivial," wrote Lafcadio Hearn from New Orleans in 1880 to his friend H. E. Krehbiel, speaking of the weird little sketches he was publishing from time to time in the columns of the *Daily Item*, the New Orleans newspaper which first gave him employment in the city where he spent the ten years from 1877 to 1887.

"But I fancy," he goes on, "that the idea of the fantastics is artistic. They are my impressions of the strange life of New Orleans. They are dreams of a tropical city. There is one twin-idea running through them all — Love and Death. And these figures embody the story of life here, as it impresses me. I hope to be able to take a trip to Mexico in the summer just to obtain literary material, sun-paint, tropical color, etc. There are tropical lilies which are venomous, but they are more beautiful than the frail and icy-white lilies of the North. Tell me if you received a fantastic founded upon the story of Ponce de Leon. I think I sent it in my last letter. I have not written any fantastics since except one — inspired by Tennyson's fancy, —

> "'My heart would hear her and beat,
>   Had it lain for a century dead —
> Would start and tremble under her feet —
>   And blossom in purple and red.'"

It was this "Fantastic," published first in the *Item* on October 21, 1880, and later re-written in more ornate style and published in the *Times-Democrat* on April 6, 1884, under the title of "L'Amour après la Mort," which is the only one of the weird little sketches that has appeared in book form, outside of those which he himself republished in *Stray Leaves from Strange Literatures*, and *Some Chinese Ghosts*.

For it was this one which he sent to a friend with the deprecatory criticism that it "belonged to the Period of Gush" and the request "to burn or tear it up after reading." He had merely enclosed it to show how and when he had first used the phrase "lentor inexpressible" to which his friend had objected.

"Fortunately his correspondent — as did most of those to whom he wrote — treasured

INTRODUCTION

everything in his handwriting," says his bi-
ographer, Mrs. Elizabeth Bisland Wetmore,
"and the fragment which bore — my impression is — the title of 'A Dead Love' (the clip-
ping lacks the caption) remains to give an example of some of the work that bears the flaws
of his 'prentice hand, before he used his tools
with the assured skill of a master." And she
quotes the strange, fanciful little sketch in full,
with the comment: "To his own, and perhaps
other middle-aged taste, 'A Dead Love' may
seem negligible, but to those still young enough,
as he himself then was, to credit passion with a
potency not only to survive 'the gradual furnace of the world,' but even to blossom in the
dust of graves, this stigmatization as 'Gush' will
seem as unfeeling as always does to the young
the dry and sapless wisdom of granddams. To
them any version of the Orphic myth is tin-
glingly credible. Yearningly desirous that the
brief flower of life may never fade, such a cry
finds an echo in the very roots of their inex-
perienced hearts. The smouldering ardor of its
style, which a chastened judgment rejected,
was perhaps less faulty than its author be-
lieved it to be in later years."

INTRODUCTION

"It was to my juvenile admiration for this particular bit of work," she goes on, "that I owed the privilege of meeting Lafcadio Hearn in the winter of 1882, and of laying the foundation of a close friendship which lasted without a break until the day of his death."

His linking of love with death in this and the other "Fantastics" was in full accord with the sombre atmosphere of the trebly stricken city to which he had come — a city with a glorious and a joyous past, but just then ruined by three horrors: — recent war, misrule under the carpet-baggers, and oft-recurring pestilence. He had come expecting much from a semi-tropical environment. He found sorrow and trouble and a wasted land; and his mood was soon in unison with the disastrous elements around him. His letter to his friend Watkin when he first came to this smitten Paradise shows how strong the impression was: "When I saw it first — sunrise over Louisiana — the tears sprang to my eyes. It was like young death — a dead bride crowned with orange flowers — a dead face that asked for a kiss. I cannot say how fair and rich and beautiful this dead South is. It has fascinated me. I

INTRODUCTION

have resolved to live in it; I could not leave it for that chill and damp Northern life again."

From the files of the *Item* and the *Times-Democrat* over a score of these "Fantastics" have been gathered, and with them certain other fanciful little sketches that seem worth preserving, though they do not deal so directly with the mystic "twin-idea of Love and Death."

In his sympathetic Introduction to Hearn's *Leaves from the Diary of an Impressionist*, Mr. Ferris Greenslet deplores the loss of that collection of these "Fantastics" made by Hearn himself as one section of the book he evidently planned to publish under the title *Ephemeræ, or Leaves from the Diary of an Impressionist*. Says Mr. Greenslet: —

"Apparently it was Hearn's intention to add to the 'Floridian Reveries' a little collection of 'Fantastics,' with such savory titles as 'Aïda,' 'The Devil's Carbuncle,' 'A Hemisphere in a Woman's Hair,' 'The Fool and Venus,' etc.[1]

[1] Among the papers held by Dr. Gould is a memorandum of some of the "Fantastics," thus numbered: —
1. "Aïda."
2. Hiouen-Thsang.

INTRODUCTION

"This group, however, is, unfortunately, lost. From the notebook labeled upon its cover 'Fantastics' many leaves have been cut, and there remains only the paper on 'Arabian Women.'"

But for the solitary copy of the files of the *Item*, preserved in the office of that paper, most of these earliest bits of original fantasy wrought by the shabby, eccentric young journalist, whose passion for exquisite words was so incomprehensible to the other "newspaper boys," would have been wholly lost.

"The modest *Item* goes no farther than St. Louis," wrote Hearn to Krehbiel; and it was for this little two-page paper, too insignificant

3. El Vómito.
4. The Devil's Carbuncle.
5. A Hemisphere in a Woman's Hair.
6. The Clock.
7. The Fool and Venus.
8. The Stranger.

Two of these — "Aïda" and "Hiouen-Thsang" — were published under those titles. Some of the others we think we have identified among the pieces entitled simply "Fantastics" at the time of their publication. "The Fool and Venus" may have been meant for what we have called "Aphrodite and the King's Prisoner." "The Clock" we have not found.

at that time to be preserved even in the city archives or in the public libraries, that he wrote most of the "tales of Love and Death" reproduced in this volume. Twenty-nine out of the thirty-odd are to be found only, so far as we know, in the brittle yellow pages of bound volumes of the *City Item*, from June, 1878, to December, 1881, to which we have been given access through the courtesy of the present owners of the *New Orleans Item*. The other six, some of which were rearrangements and paraphrases of earlier "Fantastics," appeared in the *Times-Democrat*, of which several nearly complete files exist in libraries.

Among these thirty-five brief but vitally imaginative sketches several are far superior to "L'Amour après la Mort."

The "Fantastics" proper and the "Other Fancies" have been grouped indiscriminately in chronological order, though differing greatly in spirit and in excellence of style. "The Little Red Kitten" and "At the Cemetery" are less labored in point of diction; but they are charming in their simplicity and unaffected tenderness. In the earlier of these little pictures his sympathy with our "poor brothers" — in this

9

INTRODUCTION

case "sisters" — of the animal world, from first to last a striking trait in his character, is beautifully expressed. There is delicate humor, too, as well as pathos, in the sketch. In the latter we have the glow of his feeling for the sorrow of a child, and the spring of his wonderful imagination which a few handfuls of sand not native to the spot evoke. In neither is there the least trace of the weird which is in so large a degree characteristic of most of the others. Slight as they are in texture, they seem to me to rise far above the more subtle and fanciful tales in the strength and beauty of simple truth to nature — to the best that was in his own nature.

But the others, notably "The Black Cupid," "The Undying One," "Aphrodite and the King's Prisoner," "The Fountain of Gold," "The Gypsy's Story," are not to be undervalued. There is a power of vision, an imaginative magnificence, a weird melody of word-music in them that grips the mind of the reader as in a vise.

"The Fountain of Gold" was later reproduced in the form of "A Tropical Intermezzo," recently given to a wider public in the pages

INTRODUCTION

of *Leaves from the Diary of an Impressionist.*
It is interesting to compare the first sketch
with the finished picture. The earlier work is
less dramatic, less convincing, less artistic,
though full of a charm of its own. The whole
design is transmuted into something immensely
effective by the simple device of antiquating the
language of him who tells the tale.

In a less degree the same thing may be
remarked in the comparison of "A Dead
Love," written for the *Item*, and "L'Amour
après la Mort," contributed to the *Times-
Democrat.*

In "The Tale of a Fan" may be traced, it
seems to me, the germ of what he later ex-
panded or meant to expand into "A Hemisphere in a Woman's Hair," which has not been
found.

But it is not alone the charm that clings
about all that is weird and fanciful that gives
value to this early work of Hearn's. It sheds
rich light upon one phase of his development
and forms an essential part of his biography;
and it helps to furnish proof, along with much
else of varying form and excellence, that he put
forth a vast deal of literary effort in the years

of his stay in New Orleans before his engagement with the *Times-Democrat*.

The extent and value of his work as literary editor of the *Item* has been wholly ignored by his biographers and critics. This is due largely to the fact that the matter he selected for publication in his earlier literary career was drawn from the *Times-Democrat*. But to those who have gone carefully over the files of the *Item* it is evident that he did far more original work for that paper than for the other. His forte was supposed by the editors of the *Times-Democrat* to be translation, and, with the exception of some striking editorials, his work for that paper was mostly translation. Even the *Stray Leaves from Strange Literatures* and *Some Chinese Ghosts* belong to that category.

Besides the "Fantastics," he wrote for the *Item* many editorials on a variety of subjects and many book reviews, dramatic criticisms, and translations both from the French and the Spanish, as well as Creole sketches and certain fanciful squibs illustrated with quaint original designs distinctly akin to those that appear in *Letters from the Raven*.

But unquestionably his most remarkable

INTRODUCTION

contributions to the *Item* were the "Fantastics."

From a hint given him by a traveler's tale, by a trivial street incident, by a couplet of verse, or a carven cameo in an antique shop, by an old legend, or a few grains of sand, his genius was able to create a series of vivid and mystical visions, more real to him and to his readers than the political contests or the personal gossip which fill the surrounding columns of print.

To discover these vibrant bits of poesy in their commonplace setting is like finding rare and glorious orchids in the midst of the crowfoots and black-eyed Susans that crowd the banquettes and gutters' edges of our New Orleans streets.

"He hated the routine work, and was really quite lazy about it," testifies Colonel John W. Fairfax, former owner of the *Item*, and Hearn's first New Orleans employer and friend. At the age of seventy-two this genial old gentleman recalls many incidents of his association with the eccentric young literary editor who for three years and a half aided him and Mark F. Bigney in the task of filling the columns of the unpretentious little paper which he had purchased from the printers and tramp journalists who were its original owners — for the *Item* was started on a coöperative, profit-sharing basis.

"Hearn was really quite lazy about his regular work," Colonel Fairfax insists. "We had to prod him up all the time — stick pins in him, so to speak. But when he would write one of his own little fanciful things, out of his own head — dreams — he was always dreaming — why, then he would work like mad. And people always noticed those little things of his, somehow, for they were truly lovely, wonderful. 'Fantastics' he called them."

It was Colonel Fairfax who deserves the credit of "discovering" Hearn in New Orleans, when he applied, shabby and half-starved, at the *Item* office for a job, just after he had written to his friend Watkin, June 14, 1878: "Have been here seven months and never made one cent in the city. No possible prospect of doing anything in this town now or within twenty-five years."

But his next letter (undated) says — and it is evident that the impression he had made had secured him more than he had asked for:

INTRODUCTION

"The day after I wrote you, I got a position (without asking for it) as assistant editor on the *Item*, at a salary considerably smaller than that I received on the *Commercial*, but large enough to enable me to save half of it."

And the old gentleman appears still to regard the Hearn he recalls with the sort of half-admiring, half-contemptuous, wholly marveling affection which a fine healthy turkey-cock would feel for the "ugly duckling" just beginning to reveal himself of the breed of swans.

Apparently he and Bigney allowed Hearn considerable latitude in his choice and treatment of subject. The three years of his work in their employ show bolder and more varied editorial comment, as well as five or six times as many "Fantastics" as are to be found in the six years of his work under the Bakers, and prove that the quality of his work was already fine enough to justify Page Baker's choice of him for a place on the staff of "the new literary venture."

How these strange little blossoms of Hearn's genius attracted the admiration of lovers of beauty and won him fame and friends among professional men and scholars is told most vividly in the words of Dr. Rudolph Matas, now a surgeon of international reputation, who was Hearn's friend and early foresaw his fame.

"In those days," says he, "I was not so busy as I am now, and had more time to read the books I enjoyed, and to spend long hours in talk with Hearn.

"It was in the early eighties, I remember, that I knew him first. Whitney, of the *Times-Democrat*, was a friend of mine, and I asked him one day: 'Who writes those wonderful things — translations, weird sketches, and remarkable editorials — in your paper?' And he told me, 'A queer little chap, very shy — but I'll manage for you to meet him.'

"I became editor of the *New Orleans Medical and Surgical Journal* in 1883, and it must have been shortly before this that I first met Hearn. He was astonished to find that I knew him so well — but then, you see, I had been reading these 'Fantastics' and his wonderful book-reviews and translations, and his editorials on all sorts of unusual subjects, for a long time.

"He often came to me to get information about medical points which he needed in some of his work. He was deeply interested in Ara-

INTRODUCTION

bian studies at that time, and I was able to give him some curious facts about the practice of medicine among the Arabs, which happened to be exactly what he was seeking. Not only did he read every book on Arabia which he could find, but he actually practiced the Arabic script, and he used to write me fantastic notes, addressing me as if I had been an Arab chief.

"His capacity for reading swiftly — for getting the heart out of a book — was amazing. While others read sentences, he read paragraphs, chapters — in the time it would take an ordinary reader to finish a chapter, he would have read the whole book. And this in spite of his defective vision. With his one great nearsighted eye roving over the page, he seemed to absorb the meaning of the author —to reach his thought and divine his message with incredible rapidity. He knew books so well — knew the habits of thought of their writers, the mechanics of literature. His power of analysis was intuitive. Swiftly as he read, it would be found on questioning him afterward that nothing worth while had been overlooked, and he could refer back and find any passage unerringly.

17

INTRODUCTION

"Both in taste and temperament he was morbid, and in many respects abnormal — in the great development of his genius in certain directions, and also in his limitations and deficiencies in other lines. His nature towered like a cloud-topping mountain on one side, while on others it was not only undeveloped — it was a cavity! I understood this better, perhaps, than others of his friends, knowing as I did the pathology of such natures, and for that reason our intercourse was singularly free and candid, for Hearn revealed himself to me with a frankness and unconventionality which would have startled another. I never judged him by conventional standards. I listened to the brilliant, erratic, intemperate outpourings of his mind, aware of his eccentricities without allowing them to blind me to the beauty and value of his really marvelous nature. For example, he would bitterly denounce his enemies — or fancied enemies — for he had an obsession of persecution — in language that was frightful to listen to — inventing unheard-of tortures for those whom he deemed plotters against him. Yet in reality he was as gentle and as tender-hearted as a woman — and as passionately affectionate. But there was an almost feminine jealousy in his nature, too, and a sensitiveness that was exaggerated to a degree that caused him untold suffering. He was singularly and unaffectedly modest about his work — curiously anxious to know the real opinion of those whose judgment he valued, on any work which he had done, while impatient of flattery or 'lionizing.' Yet with all his modesty he had, even in those days of his first successes, a high and proud respect for his work. He was too good a critic not to know his value; and he consistently refused to cheapen it by allowing it to appear in any second-rate medium — I mean, any of his literary work, as distinct from the journalistic matter he did for his daily bread. Nor would he lower himself by criticizing any book or poem which he did not consider worthy of his opinion. Thus he was obliged, in spite of his kind nature, which impelled him to do anything which a friend might ask, to refuse to criticize books of inferior worth, and he was very firm and dignified about such refusals. He would not debase his pen by using it on inferior subjects.

"At the time when I knew him best, he was

already highly esteemed by many who appreciated his great gifts, while others regarded him with some jealousy and would gladly have seen him put down. From the first I recognized hi' genius so clearly that he used to laugh at me foɪ my faith in his future fame. For I would often predict that he would be known to future generations as one of the great writers of the century, though it was easy to foresee that he would not receive full recognition in his life-time.

"And though he used to smile at my enthusiasm, he himself felt, I am convinced, the same certainty as to the quality of his gift, the ultimate fame that Fate held for him. It was this that made him regard his work with a reverent humility, and it was this that accounted in some degree for his extraordinary shyness, which made him shrink from being lionized or exploited by those who, at that time, would have been glad enough to entertain him and make much of him, for he had already begun to be quite an important literary person in the circles here which cared for such matters.

"But Hearn fled from social attentions as from the plague. He was by nature suspicious and he loathed flattery and pretense.

INTRODUCTION

"His sense of literary and artistic values was singularly sure, and it has always seemed to me that it was intuitive — a sort of instinctive feeling for beauty and truth.

"When he became acquainted with the work of Herbert Spencer, — through the enthusiasm of his friend Ernest Crosby for that philosopher and for the Darwinian theory of evolution, which we were all discussing with deep interest at that time — he used that thinker's philosophy as a foundation upon which to base his marvelous speculations as to the ultimate development of the race and the infinite truths of the universe. I used to listen in wonder while he talked by the hour along these lines, weaving the most beautiful and imaginative visions of what might be. For his theory of the universe was essentially literary rather than philosophical."

It was to Dr. Matas that "Chita" was dedicated, not only as a token of the warm admiration and affection which the sensitive soul of Hearn felt for the broad-minded young physician, but as an acknowledgment of the help Dr. Matas had given him in gathering the material for the setting of the story. The physician's cosmopolitan rearing and his scattered practice among French, Spanish, and even Filipino settlers in the region about Grand' Isle enabled him to give Hearn in each instance the appropriate phraseology in the dialect of the people he was writing about.

Some of the "Other Fancies" are noteworthy for special reasons. In "A River Reverie" one gets an odd glimpse of Mark Twain reflected in the personality of the dream-haunted Irish-Greek, who handles the visit of the humorist in so unjournalistic a way. How ruthlessly his recollections of the old river-captain would be excised by the copy-reader of the modern newspaper!

In several of these sketches Hearn gives a picture of the horrors of yellow fever which shows even more clearly than his letters how vivid was the impression made on him by that summer of 1878, when he passed through the epidemic with only an attack of the dengue, a mild form of the tropical plague.

Others of these sketches show the influence of contact with Spanish friends and acquaintances, and the strong longing for the tropics, which seems to have lasted all his life.

INTRODUCTION

"Aïda" is, of course, merely the story of the well-known opera by Verdi. Hearn wrote for the *Item*, during the opera season of 1880, brief outlines like this of the stories of several of the operas played at the French Opera House that winter: this one is included in this volume only because it is mentioned among the "Fantastics" in the list given in Dr. George Gould's book, *Concerning Lafcadio Hearn*. "Hiouen-Thsang" is included for the same reason, as it is not strictly a "Fantastic."

"The Devil's Carbuncle," besides being a translation, is not a "Fantastic," according to Hearn's definition of the term: it is not a story of love and death; it is a story of greed and death.

"The Post-Office" is much more breezy and out-of-doors than any of the "Fantastics," and does not properly belong with them; but it is so charming a sketch of his visit to Grand' Isle, the place which gave him the material for his first successful original story, "Chita," that it seems worth while to reproduce it.

It has been almost a commonplace, with writers treating of Hearn's development, to date from this visit the beginnings of his interest in far-away lands. But they mistake in assigning a late date for his delight in the tropics and his longing for Japan. His articles in the *Item* years before go to show that from the first it was almost an instinct with him to yearn for glimpses of the Orient and the Spanish Main. Throughout the volume of the *Item* for 1879 the column headed "Odds and Ends" reveals his interest in Spanish-American countries. It is generally shown in translated citations or quotations from *La Raza Latina*.

In finding these cameo-like studies buried in the pages of the newspapers of a generation ago, and in identifying them beyond question as Hearn's, I have been aided by Mr. John S. Kendall and by my daughter, Ethel Hutson, who have been for some years gathering traces of Hearn's journalistic activities in New Orleans. To Mr. C. G. Stith, of the *New Orleans Item*, we are indebted for the finding of the first two or three of the "Fantastics" in that paper, after we had located Hearn's work in the *Times-Democrat*.

To one who has studied his way of expressing himself in his imaginative writings the internal evidence would be quite enough to prove that

INTRODUCTION

these "Fantastics" were woven in the brain-cells of Lafcadio Hearn. But in addition to this we have the avowal of the editor-in-chief of the *Item*, elicited by the praise of the *Claiborne Guardian*.[1]

[1] In the issue of Sunday evening, September 19, 1880, appears this excerpt, with the editor's comment: —

" FANTASTICS

"*Claiborne Guardian.*

"We do not remember to have ever read a series of more brilliant articles than those which occasionally appear under the above heading in that bright little paper THE CITY ITEM. The writer, with a perfect command of the language, unites a vivid imagination. His fancy is as exuberant as the growth of tropical flowers, and is as pleasing as glowing and fascinating. We always turn to the editorial page for 'Fantastics' when we receive the ITEM. Would it be out of place to inquire who this rare genius is? It can't be that grave and dignified gentleman, M. F. Bigney. We have read many excellent sketches from his pen, but never anything like these pieces. Who is the writer that adds another to the many attractions of our prosperous and worthy exchange?"

"We gladly comply," replies the ITEM editorially, "with the request of our appreciative Claiborne contemporary. The writer of 'Fantastics' is Mr. Lafcadio Hearne [*sic*], who has been our assistant co-laborer for nearly three years. — ED. ITEM."

INTRODUCTION

The author named them only "Fantastics." We have given to each its separate title, as indicated by the most striking feature in the story. To the "Other Fancies," which we have included in the collection, he gave the titles under which they now appear, and some of them he signed.

Charles Woodward Hutson.

FANTASTICS AND OTHER FANCIES

FANTASTICS
AND OTHER FANCIES

ALL IN WHITE [1]

"No," he said, "I did not stay long in Havana. I should think it would be a terrible place to live in. Somehow, in spite of all the tropical brightness, the city gave me the idea of a huge sepulchre at times. One feels in those narrow streets as though entombed. Pretty women? — I suppose so, yes; but I saw only one. It was in one of the quaint streets which make you think that the Spaniards learned to build their cities from the Moors, — a chasm between lofty buildings, and balconies jutting out above to break the view of the narrow strip of blue sky. Nobody was in the street except myself; and the murmur of the city's life seemed to come from afar, like a ghostly whisper. The silence was so strange that I felt as if walking on the pavement of a church, and disturbing the religious quiet with my footsteps.

[1] *Item*, September 14, 1879.

FANTASTICS

I stopped before a great window — no glass, but iron bars only; — and behind the iron bars lay the only beautiful woman I saw in Havana by daylight. She could not have been more than eighteen, — a real Spanish beauty, — dark, bewitching, an oval face with noble features, and long eyelashes resting on the cheek. She was dead! All in white, — like the phantom bride of the German tradition, — white robes, white satin shoes, and one white tropical flower in her black hair, shining like a star. I do not know what it was; but its perfume came to me through the window, sweet and strange. The young woman, sleeping there all in white, against the darkness of the silent chamber within, fascinated me. I felt as if it was not right to look at her so long; yet I could not help it. Candles were burning at her head and feet; and in the stillness of the hot air their yellow flames did not even tremble. Suddenly I heard a heavy tramping at the end of the street. A battalion of Spanish soldiers were coming towards me. There was no means of proceeding; and I had no time to retreat. The street was so narrow that I was obliged to put my back to the wall in order to let them pass.

ALL IN WHITE

They passed in dead silence — I only heard the tread of the men, mechanically regular and heavily echoing. They were all in white. Every man looked at me as he passed by; and every look was dark, sinister, suspicious. I was anxious to escape those thousands of Spanish eyes; but I could not have done it without turning my face to the wall. I do not think one of them looked at the dead girl at all; but each one looked at me, and forced me to look at him. I dared not smile, — not one of the swarthy faces smiled. The situation became really unpleasant. It was like one of those nightmares in which you are obliged to witness an endless procession of phantoms, each one of whom compels you to look at it. If I had even heard a single *carajo Americano*, I should have felt relieved; but all passed me in dead silence. I was transpierced by the black steel of at least two thousand Spanish eyes, and every eye looked at me as if I had been detected in some awful crime. Yet why they did not look at that window instead of looking at me, I cannot tell. After they had passed, I looked an instant at the dead girl again; and it seemed to me that I saw the ghost of a smile, — a cynical, mocking

smile about her lips. She was well avenged, —
if her consecrated rest had been disturbed by
my heretic eyes. I can still smell the white
flower; and I can see even the silk stitches in
the white satin shoes, — the motionless yellow
tongues of the candles, — the thin dead face
that seemed to smile, and the thousand sinister
faces that smiled not, and dared me to smile."

THE LITTLE RED KITTEN[1]

THE kitten would have looked like a small red lion, but that its ears were positively enormous, — making the head like one of those little demons sculptured in mediæval stone-work which have wings instead of ears. It ate beefsteak and cockroaches, caterpillars and fish, chicken and butterflies, mosquito-hawks and roast mutton, hash and tumble-bugs, beetles and pigs' feet, crabs and spiders, moths and poached eggs, oysters and earthworms, ham and mice, rats and rice pudding, — until its belly became a realization of Noah's Ark. On this diet it soon acquired strength to whip all the ancient cats in the neighborhood, and also to take under its protection a pretty little salmon-colored cat of the same sex, which was too weak to defend itself and had been unmercifully mauled every night before the tawny sister enforced reform in the shady yard of the old Creole house. The red kitten was not very big, but was very solid and more agile than a monkey. Its flaming emerald eyes were always

[1] *Item*, September 24, 1879. Hearn's own title.

33

watching, and its enormous ears always on the alert; and woe to the cat who dared approach the weak little sister with hostile intentions. The two always slept together — the little speckled one resting its head upon the body of its protector; and the red kitten licked its companion every day like a mother washing her baby. Wherever the red kitten went the speckled kitten followed; they hunted all kinds of creeping things together, and even formed a criminal partnership in kitten stealing. One day they were forcibly separated; the red kitten being locked up in the closet under the stairs to keep it out of mischief during dinner hours, as it had evinced an insolent determination to steal a stuffed crab from the plate of Madame R. Thus temporarily deprived of its guide, philosopher, and friend, the speckled kitten unfortunately wandered under a rocking-chair violently agitated by a heavy gentleman who was reading the "Bee"; and with a sharp little cry of agony it gave up its gentle ghost. Everybody stopped eating; and there was a general outburst of indignation and sorrow. The heavy gentleman got very red in the face, and said he had not intended to do it. "Tonnerre d'une pipe; — nom d'un petit bonhomme!" — he might have been a little more careful! . . . An hour later the red kitten was vainly seeking its speckled companion — all ears and eyes. It uttered strange little cries, and vainly waited for the customary reply. Then it commenced to look everywhere — upstairs, downstairs, on the galleries, in the corners, among the shrubbery, never supposing in its innocent mind that a little speckled body was lying far away upon a heap of garbage and ashes. Then it became very silent; purring when offered food, but eating nothing. . . . At last a sudden thought seemed to strike it. It had never seen the great world which rumbled beyond the archway of the old courtyard; perhaps its little sister had wandered out there. So it would go and seek her. For the first time it wandered beyond the archway and saw the big world it had never seen before — miles of houses and myriads of people and great cotton-floats thundering by, and great wicked dogs which murder kittens. But the little red one crept along beside the houses in the narrow strip of shadow, sometimes trembling when the big wagons rolled past, and sometimes hiding in doorways when

35

it saw a dog, but still bravely seeking the lost
sister. . . . It came to a great wide street — five
times wider than the narrow street before the
old Creole house; and the sun was so hot, so
hot. The little creature was so tired and hungry, too. Perhaps somebody would help it to
find the way. But nobody seemed to notice the
red kitten, with its funny ears and great bright
eyes. It opened its little pink mouth and cried;
but nobody stopped. It could not understand
that. Whenever it had cried that way at home,
somebody had come to pet it. Suddenly a fire-
engine came roaring up the street, and a great
crowd of people were running after it. Then the
kitten got very, very frightened; and tried to
run out of the way, but its poor little brain was
so confused and there was so much noise and
shouting. . . . Next morning two little bodies
lay side by side on the ashes — miles away
from the old Creole house. The little tawny
kitten had found its speckled sister.

THE NIGHT OF ALL SAINTS [1]

THE Night of All Saints — a night clear and deep and filled with a glory of white moonlight.

And a low sweet Wind came up from the West, and wandered among the tombs, whispering to the Shadows.

And there were flowers among the tombs.

They looked into the face of the moon, and from them a thousand invisible perfumes arose into the night.

And the Wind blew upon the flowers until their soft eyelids began to close and their perfume grew fainter in the moonlight. And the Wind sought in vain to arouse them from the dreamless sleep into which they were sinking.

For the perfume of a flower is but the presence of its invisible soul; and the flowers drooped in the moonlight, and at the twelfth hour they closed their eyes forever and the incense of their lives passed away from them.

Then the Wind mourned awhile among the old white tombs; and whispered to the cypress

[1] *Item*, November 1, 1879.   Hearn's own title.

trees and to the Shadows, "Were not these offerings?"

And the Shadows and the cypresses bowed weirdly in mysterious reply. But the Wind asked, *To Whom?* And the Shadows kept silence with the cypresses.

Then the Wind entered like a ghost into the crannies of the white sepulchres, and whispered in the darkness, and coming forth shuddered and mourned.

And the Shadows shuddered also; and the cypresses sighed in the night.

"It is a mystery," sobbed the Wind, "and passeth my understanding. Wherefore these offerings to those who dwell in the darkness where even dreams are dead?"

But the trees and the Shadows answered not and the hollow tombs uttered no voice.

Then came a Wind out of the South, murmuring to the orange groves, and lifting the long tresses of the palms with the breath of his wings, and bearing back to the ancient place of tombs the souls of a thousand flowers. And the Wind of the South whispered to the souls of the flowers, "Answer, little spirits, answer my mourning brother."

THE NIGHT OF ALL SAINTS

And the flower-souls answered, making fragrant all the white streets of the white city of the dead: —

"We are the offerings of love bereaved to the All-loving, — the sacrifices of the fatherless to the All-father. We know not of the dead, — the Infinite secret hath not been revealed to us; — we know only that they sleep under the eye of Him who never sleeps. Thou hast seen the flowers die; but their perfumes live in the wings of the winds and sweeten all God's world. Is it not so with that fragrance of good deeds, which liveth after the deed hath been done, — or the memories of dead loves which soften the hearts of the living?"

And the cypresses together with the Shadows bowed answeringly; and the West Wind, ceasing to mourn, spread his gauzy wings in flight toward the rising of the sun.

The moon, sinking, made longer the long shadows; the South Wind caressed the cypresses, and, bearing with him ghosts of the flowers, rose in flight toward the dying fires of the stars.

THE DEVIL'S CARBUNCLE [1]

RICARDO PALMA, the Lima correspondent of *La Raza Latina*, has been collecting some curious South American traditions which date back to the Spanish Conquest. The following legend, entitled "*El Carbunclo del Diablo*," is one of these: —

WHEN Juan de la Torre, one of the celebrated *Conquistadores*, discovered and seized an immense treasure in one of the *huacas* near the city of Lima, the Spanish soldiers became seized with a veritable mania for treasure-seeking among the old forts and cemeteries of the Indians. Now there were there *ballesteros* belonging to the company of Captain Diego Gumiel, who had formed a partnership for the purpose of seeking fortunes among the *huacas* of Miraflores, and who had already spent weeks upon weeks in digging for treasure without finding the smallest article of value.

On Good Friday, in the year 1547, without any respect for the sanctity of the day, — for to human covetousness nothing is sacred, —

[1] *Item*, November 2, 1879. Hearn's own title.

the three *ballesteros*, after vainly sweating and panting all morning and afternoon, had not found anything except a mummy — not even a trinket or bit of pottery worth three *pesetas*. Thereupon they gave themselves over to the Father of Evil — cursing all the Powers of Heaven, and blaspheming so horribly that the Devil himself was obliged to stop his ears with cotton.

By this time the sun had set; and the adventurers were preparing to return to Lima, cursing the niggardly Indians for the unpardonable stupidity of not having been entombed in state upon beds of solid gold or silver, when one of the Spaniards gave the mummy so ferocious a kick that it rolled a considerable distance. A glimmering jewel dropped from the skeleton, and rolled slowly after the mummy.

"*Canario!*" cried one of the soldiers, "what kind of a taper is that? *Santa Maria!* what a glorious carbuncle!"

And he was about to walk toward the jewel, when the one who had kicked the corpse, and who was a great bully, held him back with the words: —

"Halt, comrade! May I never be sad if that

carbuncle does not belong to me; for it was I who found the mummy!

"May the Devil carry thee away! I first saw it shine, and may I die before any other shall possess it!"

"*Cepos quedos!*" thundered the third, unsheathing his sword, and making it whistle round his head. "So I am nobody?"

"*Caracolines!* not even the Devil's wife shall wring it from me," cried the bully, unsheathing his dagger.

And a tremendous fight began among the three comrades.

The following day some *Mitayos* found the dead body of one of the combatants, and the other two riddled with wounds, begging for a confessor. Before they died they related the story of the carbuncle, and told how it illumined the combat with a sinister and lurid light. But the carbuncle was never found after. Tradition ascribes its origin to the Devil; and it is said that each Good Friday night travelers may perceive its baleful rays twinkling from the *huaca* Juliana, rendered famous by this legend.

LES COULISSES [1]

SOUVENIRS OF A STRAKOSCH OPERA NIGHT

SURELY it cannot have been a poet who first inspired the popular mind with that widely spread and deeply erroneous belief that "behind the scenes" all is hollow mockery and emptiness and unsightliness; — that the comeliness of the pliant limbs which move to music before the starry row of shielded lights is due to a judicious distribution of sawdust; and that our visions of fair faces are created by the magic contained in pots of ointment and boxes of pearl powder of which the hiding-places are known only to those duly initiated into the awful mysteries of the Green Room.

No; the Curtain is assuredly the Veil which hides from unromantic eyes the mysteries of a veritable Fairy-World, — not a fairyland so clearly and sharply outlined as the artistic fantasies of Christmas picture-books, but a fairyland of misty landscapes and dim shadows and bright shapes moving through the vagueness of mystery. There is really a world of stronger en-

[1] *Item*, December 6, 1879. Hearn's own title.

43

chantment behind than before the scenes; —
all that movement of white limbs and fair faces
— that shifting of shadowy fields and plains,
those changing visions of mountain and wold,
of towers that disappear as in tales of knight-
errantry, and cottages transformed into palaces as in the "Arabian Nights" — is but a
small part of the great wizard-work nightly
wrought by invisible hands behind the Curtain. And when, through devious corridors
and dimly-lighted ways, — between rows of
chambers through whose doors one catches
sudden glimpses of the elves attiring in purple
and silver, in scarlet and gold, for the gaslit holi-
day among canvas woods and flowing brooks of
muslin, mystic, wonderful, — thou shalt arrive within the jagged borders of the Unknown
World itself to behold the Circles of bright
seats curving afar off in atmospheres of artificial light, and the Inhabitants of those Circles
become themselves involuntary Actors for the
amusement of the lesser audience, then verily
doth the charm begin. There is no disillusion
as yet. The Isis of the drama has lifted her
outer veil; but a veil yet more impenetrable remains to conceal the mystery of her face. The

44

LES COULISSES

Heart of all that Mimic Life — mimic yet warm and real — throbs about thee, but dost thou understand its pulsations? Thou art in the midst of a secret, in the innermost chamber of the witch-workers — yet the witchcraft remains. Thou hast approached too near the Fata Morgana of theatrical enchantment — all has vanished or tumbled into spectral ruin. Fragments of castles and antiquated cities — torn and uneven remnants of pictures of various centuries huddled together in mystic anachronism — surround and overshadow thee; but to comprehend that harmonious whole, thou must retire to the outer circles of the shining temple, before the tall Veil. About thee it is a world wrought of many broken worlds; — a world of picturesque ruin like the moon in heaven — a world of broken lights and shadows and haunted glooms — a wild dream — a work of goblinry. Content thyself, seek not disillusion; for to the gods of this mysterious sphere human curiosity is the greatest of abominations. Satisfy thyself with the knowledge that thou art in Fairyland; and that it is not given to mortals to learn all the ways of elves. What though the woods be mockeries, and the cas-

45

tles be thinner than Castles of Spain, and the white statues fair Emptinesses like the elf women of Northern dreams? — the elves and gnomes and fairies themselves are real and palpable and palpitant with the ruddy warmth of life.

Perhaps thou thinkest of those antique theatres — marble cups set between the breasts of sweetly-curving hills, with the cloud-frescoed dome of the Infinite for a ceiling, and for scenery nature's richest charms of purple mountain and azure sea and emerald groves of olive. But that beautiful materialism of the ancient theatre charmed not as the mystery of ours, — a mystery too delicate to suffer the eye of Day; — a mystery wrought by fairies who dare only toil by night. One sunbeam would destroy the charm of this dusky twilight world. Strange! how the mind wanders in this strange place! Yet it is easier to dream of two thousand years ago than to recollect that thou livest in the material present, — that only a painted ceiling lies between thy vision and the amethystine heaven of stars above, and that only a wall of plastered brick separates thee from the streets of New Orleans or the gardens westward where

the bananas are nodding their heads under the
moon. For the genii of this inner world are
weaving their spells about thee. Figures of
other centuries pass before thy eyes, as in the
steel mirror of a wizard: — lords of Italian
cities gorgeous as Emperor-moths, captains of
free companies booted and spurred, phantoms,
one may fancy, of fair women whose portraits
hang in the Uffizi Gallery, and prelates of the
sixteenth century. Did Macbeth's witches ever
perform greater magic than this? — a series of
tableaux after Racinet animated by some elfish
art? If the human character of the witchery
does not betray itself by a pretty anachronism! — some intermingling of the costumes of
the sixteenth century with those of the sev-
enteenth, a sacrifice of history to the beauty
of woman, — the illusion remains unbroken.
Thou art living, by magic, in the age of Lorenzo
di Medici; and is it strange that they should
address thee in the Italian tongue?

There is an earthquake of applauding, the
Circles of seats are again hidden, and this world
of canvas and paint is tumbling about thy ears.
The spell is broken for a moment by Beings
garbed in the everyday attire of the nineteenth

47

century, who have devoted themselves to the work of destruction and reconstruction, — to whom dreamers are an abomination and idlers behind the scenes a vexation of spirit. *Va t'en, inseq' de bois de lit !*

Aye, thou mayst well start! — thou hast seen her before. Where? — when? In a little French store, not very, very far from the old Creole Opera House. This enchantment of the place has transformed her into a fairy. Ah, thou marvelest that she can be so pretty; — nor Shakespeare's Viola nor Gautier's Graciosa were fairer to look upon than this dream of white grace and pliant comeliness in the garb of dead centuries. And yet another and another Creole girl, — familiar faces to the dwellers in the Quaint Places of New Orleans. What is the secret of that strange enchantment which teaches us that the modest everyday robe of black merino may be but the chrysalis-shell within which God's own butterflies are hidden?

Suddenly through the motley rout of princes and princesses, of captains and conspirators, of soldiers and priests, of courtiers and dukes, there comes a vision of white fairies; — these be the Damosels of the Pirouette. Thou mayest

48

watch them unobserved; for the other beings
heed them not; — Cophetua-like, the King in
his coronation robes is waltzing with a pretty
Peasant Girl; and like Christina of Spain, the
Queen is tête-à-tête with a soldier. The dancers give the impression of something aerial,
ethereal, volatile, — something which rests and
flies but walks not, — some species of splendid
fly with wings half-open. The vulgar Idea of
Sawdust vanishes before the reality of those
slender and pliant limbs. They are preparing
for the dance with a series of little exercises
which provoke a number of charming images
and call out all the supple graces of the figure;
— it is Atalanta preparing to pursue Hippo-
menes; it is a butterfly shaking its wings; it is
a white bird pluming itself with noiseless skill.
But when the Terpsichorean flight is over, and
the theatre shakes with applause; while the
dancers shrink panting and exhausted into
some shadowy hiding-place, breathing more
hurriedly than a wrestler after a long bout, —
thou wilt feel grateful to the humane spirits
who break the applause with kindly hisses, and
rebuke the ignorance which seeks only its own
pleasure in cries of encore.

FANTASTICS

And the Asmodean Prompter who moves the dramatic strings that agitate all these Puppets of mimic passion, whose sonorous tones penetrate all the recesses of the mysterious scenery without being heard before the footlights, resumes his faithful task; — the story of harmony and tragedy is continued by the orchestra and the singers, while a Babel of many tongues is heard among the wooden rocks and the canvas trees and the silent rivers of muslin. But little canst thou reck of the mimic opera. That is for those who sit in the outer circles. The music of the many-toned Opera of Life envelops and absorbs the soul of the stranger, — teaching him that the acting behind the Curtain is not all a mimicry of the Real, but in truth a melodrama of visible, tangible, sentient life, which must endure through many thousand scenes until that Shadow, who is stronger than Love, shall put out the lights, and ring down the vast and sable Curtain. And thus dreaming, thou findest thyself again in the streets, whitened by the moon! Lights, fairies, kings, and captains are gone. Ah! thou hast not been dreaming, friend; but the hearts of those who have beheld Fairyland are heavy.

THE STRANGER [1]

THE Italian had kept us all spellbound for
hours, while a great yellow moon was climbing
higher and higher above the leaves of the bananas that nodded weirdly at the windows.
Within the great hall a circle of attentive listeners — composed of that motley mixture of
the wanderers of all nations, such as can be
found only in New Orleans, and perhaps Mar-
seilles — sat in silence about the lamplit table,
riveted by the speaker's dark eyes and rich
voice. There was a natural music in those
tones; the stranger chanted as he spoke like a
wizard weaving a spell. And speaking to each
one in the tongue of his own land, he told them
of the Orient. For he had been a wanderer in
many lands; and afar off, touching the farther
horn of the moonlight crescent, lay awaiting
him a long, graceful vessel with a Greek name,
which would unfurl her white wings for flight
with the first ruddiness of morning.

"I see that you are a smoker," observed the
stranger to his host as he rose to go. "May I

[1] *Item*, April 17, 1880.

have the pleasure of presenting you with a Turkish pipe? I brought it from Constantinople."

It was moulded of blood-red clay after a fashion of Moresque art, and fretted about its edges with gilded work like the ornamentation girdling the minarets of a mosque. And a faint perfume, as of the gardens of Damascus, clung to its gaudy bowl, whereon were deeply stamped mysterious words in the Arabian tongue.

*
* *

The voice had long ceased to utter its musical syllables. The guests had departed; the lamps were extinguished within. A single ray of moonlight breaking through the shrubbery without fell upon a bouquet of flowers, breathing out their perfumed souls into the night. Only the host remained — dreaming of moons larger than ours, and fiercer summers; minarets white and keen, piercing a cloudless sky, and the many-fountained pleasure-places of the East. And the pipe exhaled its strange and mystical perfume, like the scented breath of a summer's night in the rose-gardens of a Sultan. Above, in deeps of amethyst, glimmered

the everlasting lamps of heaven; and from afar,
the voice of a muezzin seemed to cry, in tones
liquidly sweet as the voice of the stranger —
"All ye who are about to sleep, commend your
souls to Him who never sleeps."

Y PORQUE?[1]

"AH, *caballero*," said the Spanish lady, with a pretty play of fan and eye as she spoke, "you will not return to Mexico, the beautiful city?"

"No, *señorita*," replied the young man addressed, a handsome boy, about twenty-two years old, olive-skinned and graceful, with black curly hair, that had those bluish lights one sees in the plumage of a raven.

"*Y porque?*" asked the girl, laying aside her fan for a moment, and concentrating all the deep fire of her eyes upon his face.

The boy did not answer. He made an effort to speak, and turned his head aside. There was a momentary lull in the conversation. Suddenly he burst into tears, and left the room.

*
* *

The beautiful city! Ah! how well he remembered it! The mighty hills sleeping in their eternal winding-sheets of snow, the azure heaven and the bright lake rippled by mountain winds, the plaza and its familiar sights and

[1] *Item*, April 17, 1880.

54

sounds. *Y porque?* The question brought up all the old bright memories, and the present for the moment melted away, and the dream of a Mexican night rose in ghostliness before him.

He stood again within an ancient street, quaint with the quaintness of another century, and saw the great windows of the hospitable Spanish residence at which he had been so often received as a son. Again he heard the long chant of the *sereno* in the melancholy silence; again he saw the white stars glimmering like lamps above the towers of the cathedral. The windows were tall and large, and barred with bars of iron; and there were lights in one of them — flickering taper-lights that made moving shadows on the wall. And within the circle of the tapers, a young girl lay all in white with hands crossed upon her breast, and flowers in the dark hair. He remembered all with that terrible minuteness agony lends to observation — even how the flickering of the tapers played with the shadows of the silky eyelashes, making the lids seem to quiver, as though that heart, to which all his hopes and aims and love had been trusted, had not forever ceased to beat. Again the watchman solemnly chanted the hour of the night, with words of Spanish piety; and far in the distance that weird mountain which ancient Mexican fancy called "The White Lady," and modern popular imagination, "The Dead One," lay as a corpse with white arms crossed upon its bosom, in awful mockery of the eternal sleep.

A DREAM OF KITES [1]

LOOKING out into the clear blue of the night from one of those jutting balconies which constitute a summer luxury in the Creole city, the eye sometimes marks the thin black threads which the telegraph wires draw sharply against the sky. We observed last evening the infinitely extending lines of the vast web which the Electric Spider has spun about the world; and the innumerable wrecks of kites fluttering thereupon, like the bodies of gaudy flies— strange lines of tattered objects extending far into the horizon and tracking out the course of the electric messengers beyond the point at which the slender threads cease to remain visible.

How fantastic the forms of these poor tattered wrecks, when the uniform tint of night robs them of their color, and only defines their silhouettes against the sky! — some swinging to and fro wearily, like thin bodies of malefactors mummified by sunheat upon their gibbets — some wildly fluttering as in the agony of de-

[1] *Item*, June 18, 1880.

57

spair and death — some dancing grotesquely upon their perches like flying goblins — some like impaled birds, with death-stiffened wings, motionlessly attached to their wire snare, and glaring with painted eyes upon the scene below as in a stupor of astonishment at their untimely fate.

All these represented the destruction of childish ambitions — each the wreck of some boyish pleasure. Many were doubtless wept for, and dreamed of afterward regretfully on wet pillows. And stretching away into the paler blue of the horizon we looked upon the interminable hues of irregular dots they made against it and remembered that each little dot represented some little pang.

Then it was natural that we should meditate a little upon the vanity of the ways in which these childish losses had been borne. The little owners of the poor kites had hearts whose fibre differed more than that of the kites themselves. Some might weep, but some doubtless laughed with childish heroism, and soon forgot their loss; some doubtless thought the world was all askew, and that telegraph wires ought never to have been invented; some, considering critically the question of cause and effect, resolved as young philosophers to profit by their experience, and seek similar pleasures thereafter where telegraph wires ensnared not; while some, perhaps, profited not at all, but only made new kites and abandoned them to the roguish wind, which again traitorously delivered them up to the insatiable enemies of kites and birds.

Is it not said that the child is the father of the man?

And as we sat there in the silence with the stars burning in the purple deeps of the summer night above us, we dreamed of the kites which children of a larger growth fly in the face of heaven — toys of love and faith — toys of ambition and of folly — toys of grotesque resolve and flattering ideals — toys of vain dreams and vain expectation — the kites of human Hope, gaudy-colored or gray, richly tinseled or humbly simple — rising and soaring and tossing on the fickle winds of the world, only to become entangled at last in that mighty web of indissoluble and everlasting threads which the Weird Sisters spin for all of us.

HEREDITARY MEMORIES [1]

"I WAS observing," continued the Doctor, "that it very frequently happens that upon seeing or hearing something new for the first time, — that is, something entirely new to us, — we feel a surprise, not caused by the novelty of that which we see or hear, but by a very curious echo in the mind. I say echo. I would do better to use the word memory-echo. It seems to us, although we know positively we have never seen or heard of this new thing in our mortal lives, that we heard or saw it in some infinitely remote period. An old Latin writer considered this phenomenon to be a proof of the theory of Preëxistence. A Buddhist would tell you that the soul, through all its wanderings of a million years, retains faint memories of all it has seen or heard in each transmigration and that each of us now living in the flesh possesses dim and ghostly recollections of things heard and seen æons before our birth. That the phenomenon exists there can be no doubt. I am

[1] *Item*, July 22, 1880.

not a believer in Buddhism nor in the soul; but I attribute the existence of these vague memories to hereditary brain impressions."

"How do you mean, Doctor?" asked one of the boarders.

"Why, sir, I mean that a memory may be inherited just like a mole, a birthmark, a physical or a moral characteristic. Our brains, as a clever writer has expressed it, are like the rocks of the Sinaitic valley, all covered over with inscriptions written there by the long caravans of Thought. Each impression received upon the brain through the medium of the senses leaves there a hieroglyphic inscription, which, although invisible under the microscope, is nevertheless material and real. Why should not these hieroglyphs of the parent brain reappear in the brain of the child? — fainter and less decipherable to the eyes of the memory, yet not so faint as to be wholly lost."

There was a long silence. The moon rose higher; the bananas did not wave their leaves; the air still glowed with the heat of the dead day; and the stars in the blue above sparkled with that luminosity only known to Southern nights. Everything seemed to dream except the lights of heaven, and we dreamed also of the Infinite.

"Doctor," said a bearded stranger, who had remained silent all the evening, "I want to ask you a question. I have lived in the West Indies, New Zealand, Canada, Mexico; and I am something of a traveler. I have a good memory, too. I seldom forget the sight of a city I have visited. I remember every street and nook I have ever seen. How is it, then, that I dream continually of places which I am positive I have never seen, and hear in my sleep a tongue spoken that I have never heard while awake in any part of the world?"

The Doctor smiled. "Can you describe," he asked, "the places you see in your dreams?"

"I can, because I have dreamed of them more than a hundred times. Sometimes I do not dream of them for a year at a time; and then again I will dream of them every night for a week. And I always hear that strange tongue spoken.

"I sail to these places from a vast port, surrounded by huge wharfs of cut stone — white and even-worn by the friction of a mighty traffic. It is all sun there and light and air. There

62

are tropical fruits heaped up, and wines and oils and spices; and many people in brightly colored dresses, blue and yellow. I have a queer idea that it might be some port in the Mediterranean.

"Then I arrive after a long voyage in a strange country. I do not remember the disembarking. I only remember a great city. It is not built like any American or European city. Its houses are high; its streets narrow and fantastic. I have seen in Spain a few buildings which reminded me of those I dream about; but they were old Moorish buildings.

"There is an immense edifice in one part of the city, with two graceful domes, rising like white breasts against a sky most intensely blue. There are tall and very slender white towers near the domes. There are enormous stairways of white stone leading down into an expanse of still water, reflecting the shadows of the palace, or whatever it may be. I see birds there with immense beaks and flaming plumage, walking about near the water. I have seen such birds stuffed, but never alive, except in dreams. But I do not remember where the stuffed birds came from.

FANTASTICS

"I feel that the city is as large as one of our great Western cities here. I do not see it, but I feel it. There is a mighty current of human life flowing through its streets. The people are swarthy and graceful. They look like statues of bronze. Their features are delicate and their hair black and straight. Some of the women are naked to the waist, and exceedingly beautiful. They wear immense earrings and curious ornaments of bright metal. The men wear turbans and brightly colored dresses. Some are very lightly clad. There are so many dressed in white! All speak the same strange language I have told you of, and there are camels and apes and elephants and cattle that are not like our cattle; they have a hump between the head and shoulders."

"Is that all?" asked the Doctor.

"All I can remember."

"Were you ever in India?"

"No, sir."

"Have you never visited India even through the medium of art — books, engravings, photographs?"

"I do not believe I have ever read a single illustrated book upon India. I have seen articles brought from India, and some pictures; — drawings on rice paper; but this of very late years. I have never seen anything in pictures like the place I have described to you."

"How long have you been dreaming of these places?"

"Well, since I was a boy."

"Was your father ever in India, or your mother?"

"My father was, sir; not my mother. But he died there when I was a child. I was born in Europe."

"Hereditary impressions!" cried the Doctor. "That explains all your stories of metempsychosis. The memories of the father descending to the children, perhaps even to the third and fourth generation. You dream of Indian cities you have never seen and probably never will see. Why? Because the delicate and invisible impressions made upon the brain of an English traveler in India, through the mediums of sight and sound, are inherited by his children born in a colder climate who have never seen the Orient, and will nevertheless be forever haunted by visions of the Far East."

THE GHOSTLY KISS [1]

THE theatre was full. I cannot remember what they were playing. I did not have time to observe the actors. I only remember how vast the building seemed. Looking back, I saw an ocean of faces stretching away almost beyond the eye's power of definition to the far circles where the seats rose tier above tier in lines of illumination. The ceiling was blue, and in the midst a great mellow lamp hung suspended like a moon, at a height so lofty that I could not see the suspending chain. All the seats were black. I fancied that the theatre was hung with hangings of black velvet, bordered with a silver fringe that glimmered like tears. The audience were all in white.

All in white! — I asked myself whether I was not in some theatre of some tropical city — why all in white? I could not guess. I fancied at moments that I could perceive a moonlit landscape through far distant oriel windows, and the crests of palms casting moving shadows like gigantic spiders. The air was sweet

[1] *Item*, July 24, 1880.

66

with a strange and a new perfume; it was a drowsy air — a poppied air, in which the waving of innumerable white fans made no rustle, no sound.

There was a strange stillness and a strange silence. All eyes were turned toward the stage, except my own. I gazed in every direction but that of the stage! I cannot imagine why it was that I rarely looked toward the stage. No one noticed me; no one appeared to perceive that I was the only person in all that vast assembly clad in black — a tiny dark speck in a sea of white light.

Gradually the voices of the actors seemed to me to become fainter and fainter — thin sounds like whispers from another world — a world of ghosts! — and the music seemed not music, but only an echo in the mind of the hearer, like a memory of songs heard and forgotten in forgotten years.

There were faces that I thought strangely familiar — faces I fancied I had seen somewhere else in some other time. But none recognized me.

*
*   *.

FANTASTICS

A woman sat before me — a fair woman with
hair as brightly golden as the locks of Aphrodite. I asked my heart why it beat so strangely
when I turned my eyes upon her. I felt as if it
sought to leap from my breast and fling itself
all palpitating under her feet. I watched the
delicate movements of her neck, where a few
loose bright curls were straying, like strands of
gold clinging to a column of ivory; — the soft
curve of the cheek flushed by a faint ruddiness
like the velvet surface of a half-ripe peach; —
the grace of the curving lips — lips sweet as
those of the Cnidian Venus, which even after
two thousand years still seem humid, as with
the kisses of the last lover. But the eyes I could
not see.

And a strange desire rose within me — an
intense wish to kiss those lips. My heart said,
Yes; — my reason whispered, No. I thought
of the ten thousand thousand eyes that might
suddenly be turned upon me. I looked back;
and it seemed to me as if the whole theatre had
grown vaster! The circles of seats had re-
ceded; — the great centre lamp seemed to have
mounted higher; — the audience seemed vast
as that we dream of in visions of the Last Judg-

ment. And my heart beat so violently that I heard its passionate pulsation, louder than the voices of the actors and I feared lest it should betray me to all the host of white-clad men and women above me. But none seemed to hear or to see me. I trembled as I thought of the consequences of obeying the mad impulse that became every moment more overpowering and uncontrollable.

And my heart answered, "One kiss of those lips were worth the pain of ten thousand deaths."

*
* *

I do not remember that I arose. I only remember finding myself beside her, close to her, breathing her perfumed breath, and gazing into eyes deep as the amethystine heaven of a tropical night. I pressed my lips passionately to hers; — I felt a thrill of inexpressible delight and triumph; — I felt the warm soft lips curl back to meet mine, and give me back my kiss!

And a great fear suddenly came upon me. And all the multitude of white-clad men and women arose in silence; and ten thousand thousand eyes looked upon me.

*

*   *

I heard a voice, faint, sweet, — such a voice as we hear when dead loves visit us in dreams.

"Thou hast kissed me: the compact is sealed forever."

And raising my eyes once more I saw that all the seats were graves and all the white dresses shrouds. Above me a light still shone in the blue roof, but only the light of a white moon in the eternal azure of heaven. White tombs stretched away in weird file to the verge of the horizon; — where it had seemed to me that I beheld a play, I saw only a lofty mausoleum; — and I knew that the perfume of the night was but the breath of flowers dying upon the tombs!

THE BLACK CUPID [1]

THERE was a small picture hanging in the
room; and I took the light to examine it. I do
not know why I could not sleep. Perhaps it
was the excitement of travel.

The gilded frame, massive and richly
moulded, inclosed one of the strangest paint-
ings I had ever seen, a woman's head lying on a
velvet pillow, one arm raised and one bare
shoulder with part of a beautiful bosom relieved
against a dark background. As I said, the
painting was small. The young woman was
evidently reclining upon her right side; but
only her head, elevated upon the velvet pillow,
her white throat, one beautiful arm and part
of the bosom was visible.

With consummate art the painter had con-
trived that the spectator should feel as though
leaning over the edge of the couch — not visible in the picture — so as to bring his face close
to the beautiful face on the pillow. It was one
of the most charming heads a human being
ever dreamed of; — such a delicate bloom on

[1] *Item*, July 29, 1880.

the cheeks; — such a soft, humid light in the
half-closed eyes; — such sun-bright hair; —
such carnation lips; — such an oval outline!
And all this relieved against a deep black background. In the lobe of the left ear I noticed
a curious earring — a tiny Cupid wrought in
black jet, suspending himself by his bow, which
he held by each end, as if trying to pull it away
from the tiny gold chain which fettered it to
the beautiful ear, delicate and faintly rosy as a
seashell. What a strange earring it was! I wondered if the black Cupid presided over unlaw-
ful loves, unblest *amours!*

But the most curious thing about the picture
was the attitude and aspect of the beautiful
woman. Her head, partly thrown back, with
half-closed eyes and tender smile, seemed to
be asking a kiss. The lips pouted expectantly.
I almost fancied I could feel her perfumed
breath. Under the rounded arm I noticed a
silky floss of bright hair in tiny curls. The arm
was raised as if to be flung about the neck of the
person from whom the kiss was expected. I was
astonished by the art of the painter. No photograph could have rendered such effects, however delicately colored; no photograph could

have reproduced the gloss of the smooth shoulder, the veins, the smallest details! But the picture had a curious fascination. It produced an effect upon me as if I were looking at living beauty, a rosy and palpitating reality. Under the unsteady light of the lamp I once fancied that I saw the lips move, the eyes glisten! The head seemed to advance itself out of the canvas as though to be kissed. Perhaps it was very foolish; but I could not help kissing it — not once but a hundred times; and then I suddenly became frightened. Stories of bleeding statues and mysterious pictures and haunted tapestry came to my mind; and alone in a strange house and a strange city I felt oddly nervous. I placed the light on the table and went to bed.

But it was impossible to sleep. Whenever I began to doze a little, I saw the beautiful head on the pillow close beside me, — the same smile, the same lips, the golden hair, the silky floss under the caressing arm. I rose, dressed myself, lit a pipe, blew out the light, and smoked in the dark, until the faint blue tints of day stole in through the windows. Afar off I saw the white teeth of the Sierra flush rosily, and heard the rumbling of awakening traffic.

FANTASTICS

"*Las cinco menos quarto, señor,*" cried the servant as he knocked upon my door, — "*tiempo para levantarse.*"

*
*   *

Before leaving I asked the landlord about the picture.

He answered with a smile, "It was painted by a madman, señor."

"But who?" I asked. "Mad or not, he was a master genius."

"I do not even remember his name. He is dead. They allowed him to paint in the madhouse. It kept his mind tranquil. I obtained the painting from his family after his death. They refused to accept money for it, saying they were glad to give it away."

*
*   *

I had forgotten all about the painting when some five years after I happened to be passing through a little street in Mexico City. My attention was suddenly attracted by some articles I saw in the window of a dingy shop, kept by a

74

Spanish Jew. A pair of earrings — two little Cupids wrought in black jet, holding their bows above their heads, the bows being attached by slender gold chains to the hooks of the earrings!

I remembered the picture in a moment! And that night!

*

* *

"I do not really care to sell them, señor," said the swarthy jeweler, "unless I get my price. You cannot get another pair like them. I know who made them! They were made for an artist who came here expressly with the design. He wished to make a present to a certain woman."

"*Una Méjicana?*"

"No, *Americana.*"

"Fair, with dark eyes — about twenty, perhaps, at that time — a little rosy?"

"Why, did you know her? They used to call her Josefita. You know he killed her? Jealousy. They found her still smiling, as if she had been struck while asleep. A '*puñal.*' I got the earrings back at a sale."

"And the artist?"

FANTASTICS

"Died at P——, mad! Some say he was mad when he killed her. If you really want the earrings, I will let you have them for sixty pesos. They cost a hundred and fifty."

WHEN I WAS A FLOWER[1]

I WAS once a flower — fair and large. My snowy chalice, filled with a perfume so rich as to intoxicate the rainbow-winged insects that perched upon it, recalled to those who beheld me the beauty of those myrrhine cups used at the banquets of the old Cæsars.

The bees sang to me all through the bright summer; the winds caressed me in the hours of sultriness; the Spirit of the Dew filled my white cup by night. Great plants, with leaves broader than the ears of elephants, overshadowed me as with a canopy of living emerald.

Far off I heard the river singing its mystic and everlasting hymn and the songs of a thousand birds. By night I peeped up through my satiny petals at the infinite procession of the stars; and by day I turned forever to the eye of the sun my heart of yellow gold.

Hummingbirds with jeweled breasts, flying from the Rising of the Sun, nestled near me and drank the perfumed dews left lingering in my chalice, and sang to me of the wonders of un-

[1] *Item*, August 13, 1880.

77

known lands — of black roses that grew only in the gardens of magicians and spectral lilies whose perfume is death which open their hearts only to tropical moons.

*
*　　*

They severed the emerald thread of my life, and placed me in her hair. I did not feel the slow agony of death, like the fettered fireflies that glimmered as stars in the night-darkness of those splendid tresses. I felt the perfume of my life mingling in her blood and entering the secret chambers of her heart; and I mourned that I was but a flower.

*
*　　*

That night we passed away together. I know not how she died. I had hoped to share her eternal sleep; but a weird wind entering through the casement rent my dead leaves asunder and scattered them in white ruin upon the pillow. Yet my ghost like a faint perfume still haunted the silent chamber and hovered about the flames of the waxen tapers.

*
*　　*

WHEN I WAS A FLOWER

Other flowers, not of my race, are blooming above her place of rest. It is her blood that lives in the rosiness of their petals; her breath that lends perfume to their leaves; her life that vitalizes their veins of diaphanous green. But in the wizard hours of the night, the merciful Spirit of the Dew, who mourns the death of summer day, bears me aloft and permits me to mingle with the crystal tears which fall upon her grave.

METEMPSYCHOSIS [1]

"THOSE theories which you call wild dreams," cried the Doctor, rising to his feet as he spoke, his features glowing with enthusiasm under the moon, "are but the mystic veils with which the eternal Isis veils her awful face. Your deep German philosophy is shallow — your modern pantheism vaguer than smoke — compared with the mighty knowledge of the East. The theories of the greatest modern thinkers were taught in India before the name of Rome was heard in the world; and our scientific researches of to-day simply confirm most ancient Oriental beliefs, which we, in our ignorance, have spoken of as dreams of madmen."

" Yes, but surely, you cannot otherwise characterize the idea of the transmigration of souls? "

"Ah! souls, souls," replied the stranger, drawing at his cigar until it glowed like a car-buncle in the night, — "we have nothing to do with souls, but with facts. The metempsycho-sis is only the philosophic symbol of a vast

[1] *Item*, September 7, 1880.

natural fact, grotesque only to those who understand it not; — just as the most hideous
Indian idol, diamond-eyed and skull-chapleted,
represents to the Brahmin a hidden truth incomprehensible to the people. Conscious of the
eternity of Matter and Force; — knowing that
the substance of whirling universes, like clay
in the hands of the potter, has been and is being
and will be forever fashioned into myriad shifting forms; — knowing that shapes alone are
evanescent, and that each atom of our living
bodies has been from the beginning and will
always be, even after the mountains have
melted like wax in the heat of a world's dissolution, — it is impossible to regard the theory of
transmigration as a mere fantasy. Each particle
of our flesh has lived before our birth through
millions of transmigrations more wonderful
than any poet has dared to dream of; and the
life-force that throbs in the heart of each one
of us has throbbed for all time in the eternal
metempsychosis of the universe. Each atom
of our blood has doubtless circulated, before
our very civilization commenced, through the
veins of millions of living creatures, — soaring,
crawling, or dwelling in the depths of the sea;

and each molecule that floats in a sunbeam
has, perhaps, vibrated to the thrill of human
passion. The soil under my foot has lived and
loved; and Nature, refashioning the paste in
her awful laboratory into new forms of being,
shall make this clay to live and hope and suffer again. Dare I even whisper to you of the
past transformations of the substance of the
rosiest lips you have kissed, or the brightest eyes
which have mirrored your look? We have lived
innumerable lives in the past; we have lived in
the flowers, in the birds, in the emerald abysses
of the ocean; — we have slept in the silence of
solid rocks, and moved in the swells of the
thunder-chanting sea; — we have been women
as well as men; — we have changed our sex a
thousand times like the angels of the Talmud;
and we shall continue the everlasting transmigration long after the present universe has
passed away and the fires of the stars have
burned themselves out. Can one know these
things and laugh at the theories of the East?"

"But the theory of Cycles —"

"It is not less of a solemn truth. Knowing
that Force and Matter are eternal, we know
also that the kaleidoscope of changing shapes

82

must whirl forever. But as the colored particles within a kaleidoscope are limited, only a certain number of combinations may be produced. Are not the elements of eternal matter limited? If so, their combinations must also be; and as the everlasting force must forever continue to create forms, it can only repeat its work. Then, we must believe that all which has already happened must have happened before throughout all time, and will happen again at vast intervals through all eternity. It is not the first time we have sat together on the night of September 6; — we have done so in other Septembers, yet the same; and in other New Orleanses, the same yet not the same. We must have done it centrillions of times before, and will do it centrillions of times again through the æons of the future. I shall be again as I am, yet different; I shall smoke the same cigar, yet a different one. The same chair with the same scratches on its polished back will be there for you to sit in; and we shall hold the same conversation. The same good-natured lady will bring us a bottle of wine of the same quality; and the same persons will be reunited in this quaint Creole house. Trees like these will fling their shadows on the

pavement; and above us shall we again behold
as now the golden swarm of worlds sparkling
in the abysses of the infinite night. There will
be new stars and a new universe, yet we shall
know it only as we know it at this moment that
centrillions of years ago we must have suffered
and hoped and loved as we do in these weary
years. Good-bye, friends!''

He flung the stump of his cigar among the
vines, where it expired in a shower of rosy
sparks; and his footsteps died away forever.
NAY, not forever; for though we should see him
no more in this life, shall we not see him again
throughout the Cycles and the Æons? YEA,
alas, forever; for even though we should see
him again throughout the Cycles and the Æons,
will it not be so that he always departeth under
the same circumstances and at the same moment, *in sæcula sæculorum?*

THE UNDYING ONE [1]

I have lived for three thousand years; I am weary of men and of the world: this earth has become too small for such as I; this sky seems a gray vault of lead about to sink down and crush me.

There is not a silver hair in my head; the dust of thirty centuries has not dimmed my eyes. Yet I am weary of the earth.

I speak a thousand tongues; and the faces of the continents are familiar to me as the characters of a book; the heavens have unrolled themselves before mine eyes as a scroll; and the entrails of the earth have no secrets for me.

I have sought knowledge in the deepest deeps of ocean gulfs; — in the waste places where sands shift their yellow waves, with a dry and bony sound; — in the corruption of charnel houses and the hidden horrors of the catacombs; — amid the virgin snows of Dwalagiri; — in the awful labyrinths of forests untrodden by man; — in the wombs of dead volcanoes; — in lands where the surface of lake or stream is

[1] *Item*, September 18, 1880.

studded with the backs of hippopotami or enameled with the mail of crocodiles; — at the extremities of the world where spectral glaciers float over inky seas; — in those strange parts where no life is, where the mountains are rent asunder by throes of primeval earthquake, and where the eyes behold only a world of parched and jagged ruin, like the Moon — of dried-up seas and river channels worn out by torrents that ceased to roll long ere the birth of man.

All the knowledge of all the centuries, all the craft and skill and cunning of man in all things — are mine, and yet more!

For Life and Death have whispered me their most ancient secrets; and all that men have vainly sought to learn has for me no mystery.

Have I not tasted all the pleasures of this petty world, — pleasures that would have consumed to ashes a frame less mighty than my own?

I have built temples with the Egyptians, the princes of India, and the Cæsars; — I have aided conquerors to vanquish a world; — I have reveled through nights of orgiastic fury with rulers of Thebes and Babylon; — I have been drunk with wine and blood!

THE UNDYING ONE

The kingdoms of the earth and all their riches and glory have been mine.

With that lever which Archimedes desired I have uplifted empires and overthrown dynasties. Nay! like a god, I have held the world in the hollow of my hand.

All that the beauty of youth and the love of woman can give to make joyful the hearts of men, have I possessed; — no Assyrian king, no Solomon, no ruler of Samarcand, no Caliph of Bagdad, no Rajah of the most eastern East, has ever loved as I; and in my myriad loves I have beheld the realization of all that human thought had conceived or human heart desired or human hand crystallized into that marble of Pentelicus called imperishable, — yet less enduring than these iron limbs of mine.

And ruddy I remain like that rosy granite of Egypt on which kings carved their dreams of eternity.

But I am weary of this world!

I have attained all that I sought; I have desired nothing that I have not obtained — save that I now vainly desire and yet shall never obtain.

There is no comrade for me in all this earth;

no mind that can comprehend me; no heart that can love me for what I am.

Should I utter what I know, no living creature could understand; should I write my knowledge no human brain could grasp my thought. Wearing the shape of a man, capable of doing all that man can do, — yet more perfectly than man can ever do, — I must live as these my frail companions, and descend to the level of their feeble minds, and imitate their puny works, though owning the wisdom of a god! How mad were those Greek dreamers who sang of gods descending to the level of humanity that they might love a woman!

In other centuries I feared to beget a son, — a son to whom I might have bequeathed my own immortal youth; — jealous that I was of sharing my secret with any terrestrial creature! Now the time has past. No son of mine born in this age, of this degenerate race, could ever become a worthy companion for me. Oceans would change their beds, and new continents arise from the emerald gulfs, and new races appear upon the earth ere he could comprehend the least of my thoughts!

The future holds no pleasure in reserve for

me: — I have foreseen the phases of a myriad
million years. All that has been will be again:
— all that will be has been before. I am solitary as one in a desert; for men have become as
puppets in my eyes, and the voice of living
woman hath no sweetness for my ears.

Only to the voices of the winds and of the sea
do I hearken; — yet do even these weary me,
for they murmured me the same music and
chanted me the same hymns, among aged
woods or ancient rocks, three thousand years
ago!

To-night I shall have seen the moon wax and
wane thirty-six thousand nine hundred times!
And my eyes are weary of gazing upon its white
face.

Ah! I might be willing to live on through endless years, could I but transport myself to other
glittering worlds, illuminated by double suns
and encircled by galaxies of huge moons! —
other worlds in which I might find knowledge
equal to my own, and minds worthy of my com-
panionship, — and — perhaps — women that
I might love, — not hollow Emptinesses, not
El-women like the spectres of Scandinavian
fable, and like the frail mothers of this puny

terrestrial race, but creatures of immortal beauty worthy to create immortal children!

Alas! — there is a power mightier than my will, deeper than my knowledge, — a Force "deaf as fire, blind as the night," which binds me forever to this world of men.

Must I remain like Prometheus chained to his rock in never-ceasing pain, with vitals eternally gnawed by the sharp beak of the vulture of Despair, or dissolve this glorious body of mine forever?

I might live till the sun grows dim and cold; yet am I too weary to live longer.

I shall die utterly, — even as the beast dieth, even as the poorest being dieth that bears the shape of man; and leave no written thought behind that human thought can ever grasp. I shall pass away as a flying smoke, as a shadow, as a bubble in the crest of a wave in mid-ocean, as the flame of a taper blown out; and none shall ever know that which I was. This heart that has beaten unceasingly for three thousand years; these feet that have trod the soil of all parts of the earth; these hands that have moulded the destinies of nations; this brain that contains a thousandfold more wisdom than all the children of the earth ever knew, shall soon cease to be. And yet to shatter and destroy the wondrous mechanism of this brain — a brain worthy of the gods men dream of — a temple in which all the archives of terrestrial knowledge are stored!

.   .   .   .

The moon is up! O death-white dead world! — couldst thou too feel, how gladly wouldst thou cease thy corpselike circlings in the Night of Immensity and follow me to that darker immensity where even dreams are dead!

THE VISION OF THE DEAD CREOLE [1]

THE waters of the Gulf were tepid in the warmth of the tropical night. A huge moon looked down upon me as I swam toward the palm-fringed beach; and looking back I saw the rigging of the vessel sharply cut against its bright face. There was no sound! The sea-ripples kissed the brown sands silently, as if afraid; faint breezes laden with odors of saffron and cinnamon and drowsy flowers came over the water; — the stars seemed vaster than in other nights; — the fires of the Southern Cross burned steadily without one diamond-twinkle; — I paused a moment in terror; — for it seemed I could hear the night breathe — in long, weird sighs. The fancy passed as quickly as it came. The ship's bells struck the first hour of the morning. I stood again on the shore where I had played as a child, and saw through the palms the pale houses of the quaint city beyond, whence I had fled with

[1] *Item*, September 25, 1880.

blood upon my hands twenty-seven long years
before.

*
*   *

Was it a witch-night, that the city slumbered so deep a sleep and the *sereno* slept at his
post as I passed? I know not, but it was well
for him that he slept! I passed noiselessly as
the Shadow of Death through the ancient gates,
and through the shadows flung down by the
projecting balconies, and along the side of the
plaza unilluminated by the gaze of the tropical
moon, and where the towers of the cathedral
made goblin shapes of darkness on the pavement; and along narrow ways where the star-
sprinkled blue of heaven above seemed but a
ribbon of azure, jagged and gashed along its
edges by sharp projections of balconies; and
beyond again into the white moonshine, where
orange trees filled the warm air with a perfume
as that of a nuptial chamber; and beyond, yet
farther, where ancient cypresses with roots and
branches gnarled and twisted as by the tortures
of a thousand years of agony, bowed weirdly
over the Place of Tombs.

*
*   *

FANTASTICS

Gigantic spiders spun their webs under the moon between the walls of the tombs; — vipers glided over my feet; — the vampire hovered above under the stars; and fireflies like corpse-lights circled about the resting-places of the dead. Great vines embraced the marbles green with fungus-growths; — the ivy buried its lizard feet in the stones; — *lianas* had woven a veil, thick as that of Isis, across the epitaphs carven above the graves. But I found HER tomb! I would have reached it, as I had sworn, even in the teeth of Death and Hell!

I tore asunder the venomous plants which clung to the marble like reptiles; — but the blood poured from my hands upon her name; — and I could not find one unreddened spot to kiss. And I heard the blood from my fingers dripping with a thick, dead sound, as of molten lead, upon the leaves of the uptorn plants at my feet.

*
* *

And the dead years rose from their graves of mist and stood around me! I saw the moss-green terrace where I received her first kiss that filled my veins with madness; — the marble

THE VISION OF THE DEAD CREOLE

urns with their carved bas-reliefs of naked dancing boys; —the dead fountain choked with
water-lilies; — the monstrous flowers that
opened their hearts to the moon. And SHE! —
the sinuous outlines of that body of Corinthian
bronze unconcealed by the feathery lightness of
the white robe she wore; — the Creole eyes; —
the pouting and passionate mouth; — and that
cruel, sphinx-smile, that smile of Egypt, eternally pitiless, eternally mystical, — the smile
she wore when I flung myself like a worm before
her to kiss her feet, and vainly shrieked to her
to trample upon me, to spit upon me! And after
my fierce moment of vengeance, the smile of
Egypt still remained upon her dark face, as
though moulded in everlasting bronze.

*
* *

There was no rustle among the *lianas*, no stir
among the dead leaves; yet SHE stood again before me! My heart seemed to cease its beatings;
— a chill as of those nights in which I had sailed
Antarctic seas passed over me! Robed in white
as in the buried years, with lights like fireflies
in her hair, and the same dark, elfish smile!

95

And suddenly the chill passed away with a fierce cataclysm of the blood, as though each of its cells were heated by volcanic fire; — for the strange words of the Hebrew canticle came to me like a far echo, —

LOVE IS STRONG AS DEATH!

I burst the fetters with which horror had chained my voice; — I spake to her; I wept, — I wept tears of blood!

And the old voice came to me, argentine and low and mockingly sweet as the voices of birds that call to each other through the fervid West Indian night, —

"I knew thou wouldst come back to me, — howsoever long thou mightst wander under other skies and over other seas.

"Didst thou dream that I was dead? Nay, I die not so quickly! I have lived through all these years. I shall live on; and thou must return hither again to visit me like a thief in the night.

"Knowest thou how I have lived? I have lived in the bitter tears thou hast wept through all these long years; — the agony of the remorse that seized thee in silent nights and lonesome wastes; — in the breath of thy youth and life exhaled in passionate agony when no human eyes beheld thee; — in the images that haunt thy dreams and make it a horror for thee to find thyself alone! Yet wouldst thou kiss me —"

I looked upon her again in the white light; — I saw the same weirdly beautiful face, the same smile of the sphinx; — I saw the vacant tomb yawning to its entrails; — I saw its shadow — my shadow — lying sharply upon the graves; — and I saw that the tall white figure before me *cast no shadow before the moon!*

And suddenly under the stars, sonorous and vibrant as far cathedral bells, the voices of the awakening watchmen chanted, — *Ave Maria Purísima! — las tres de la mañana, y tiempo sereno!*

THE NAME ON THE STONE[1]

"As surely as the wild bird seeks the summer, you will come back," she whispered. "Is there a drop of blood in your veins that does not grow ruddier and warmer at the thought of me? Does not your heart beat quicker at this moment because I am here? It belongs to me; — it obeys me in spite of your feeble will; — it will remain my slave when you are gone. You have bewitched yourself at my lips; I hold you as a bird is held by an invisible thread; and my thread, invisible and intangible, is stronger than your will. Fly: but you can no longer fly beyond the circle in which my wish confines you. Go: but I shall come to you in dreams of the night; and you will be awakened by the beating of your own heart to find yourself alone with darkness and memory. Sleep in whose arms you will, I shall come like a ghost between you; kiss a thousand lips, but it will be I that shall receive them. Though you circle the earth in your wanderings, you will never be able to leave my memory behind you; and your

[1] *Item*, October 9, 1880.

pulse will quicken at recollections of me whether you find yourself under Indian suns or Northern lights. You lie when you say you do not love me! — your heart would fling itself under my feet could it escape from its living prison! You will come back."

* *
* *

And having vainly sought rest through many vainly spent years, I returned to her. It was a night of wild winds and fleeting shadows and strange clouds that fled like phantoms before the storm and across the face of the moon. "You are a cursed witch," I shrieked, "but I have come back!"

And she, placing a finger — white as the waxen tapers that are burned at the feet of the dead — upon my lips, only smiled and whispered, "Come with me."

And I followed her.

The thunder muttered in the east; the horizon pulsated with lightnings; the night-birds screamed as we reached the iron gates of the burial-ground, which swung open with a groan at her touch.

Noiselessly she passed through the ranges of the graves; and I saw the mounds flame when her feet touched them, — flame with a cold white dead flame like the fire of the glow-worm.

Was it an illusion of broken moonlight and flying clouds, or did the dead rise and follow us like a bridal train?

And was it only the vibration of the thunder, or did the earth quake when I stood upon *that* grave?

"Look not behind you even for an instant," she muttered, "or you are lost."

*
* *

But there came to me a strange desire to read the name graven upon the moss-darkened stone; and even as it came the storm unveiled the face of the moon.

And the dark shadow at my side whispered, "Read it not!"

And the moon veiled herself again. "I cannot go! I cannot go!" I whispered passionately, "until I have read the name upon this stone."

Then a flash of lightning in the east revealed

THE NAME ON THE STONE

to me the name; and an agony of memory came
upon me; and I shrieked it to the flying clouds
and the wan lights of heaven!

Again the earth quaked under my feet; and
a white Shape rose from the bosom of the grave
like an exhalation and stood before me: I felt
the caress of lips shadowy as those of the fair
phantom women who haunt the dreams of
youth; and the echo of a dead voice, faint as
the whisper of a summer wind, murmured: —
"Love, love is stronger than Death! — I come
back from the eternal night to save thee!"

APHRODITE AND THE KING'S PRISONER [1]

COLUMNS of Corinthian marble stretching away in mighty perspective and rearing their acanthus capitals a hundred feet above the polished marble from which they rose; — antique mosaics from the years of Hadrian; — Pompeiian frescoes limning all the sacrifices made to Aphrodite; — naked bronzes uplifting marvelous candelabra; — fantastically beautiful oddities in terra cotta; — miracles of art in Pentelic marble; — tripods supporting vessels of burning spices which filled the palace with perfumes as intoxicating as the Song of Solomon; — and in the midst of all a range of melodious fountains amid whose waters white nymphs showed their smooth thighs of stone and curved their marble figures into all the postures that harmonize with beauty. Vast gardens of myrtle and groves of laurel, mystic and shadowy as those of Daphne, surrounded the palace with a world of deep green,

[1] *Item*, October 12, 1880.

broken only at intervals by the whiteness of
Parian dryads; — flowers formed a living car-
pet upon the breadth of the terraces, and a
river washed the eastern walls and marble
stairways of the edifice. It was a world of
wonders and of marvels, of riches and rarities,
though created by the vengeance of a king.
There was but one human life amid all that
enchantment of Greek marble, of petrified
loveliness and beauty made motionless in
bronze. No servants were ever seen; — no
voice was ever heard; — there was no exit from
that strange paradise. It was said that the
king's prisoner was served by invisible hands;
— that tables covered with luxurious viands
rose up through the marble pavements at
regular hours; — and the fumes of the richest
wines of the Levant, sweetened with honey,
perfumed the chamber chosen for his repasts.
All that art could inspire, all that gold might
obtain, all that the wealth of a world could create were for him, — save only the sound of a
human voice and the sight of a human face.
To madden in the presence of unattainable
loveliness, to consume his heart in wild longings to realize the ravishing myth of Pygma-

lion, to die of a dream of beauty, — such was
the sentence of the king!

*

*　　*

Lovelier than all other lovelinesses created in
stone or gem or eternal bronze by the hands of
men whose lives were burnt out in longings for a
living idol worthy of their dreams of perfect
beauty — a figure of Aphrodite displayed the
infinite harmony of her naked loveliness upon
a pedestal of black marble, so broad and so
highly polished that it reflected the divine
poem of her body like a mirror of ebony — the
Foam-born rising from the silent deeps of a
black Ægean. The delicate mellowness of the
antique marble admirably mocked the tint of
human flesh; — a tropical glow, a golden
warmth seemed to fill the motionless miracle —
this dream of love frozen into marble by a
genius greater than Praxiteles; no modern re-
storer had given to the attitude of this bright
divinity the Christian anachronism of shame.
With arms extended as if to welcome a lover,
all the exquisite curves of her bosom faced
the eyes of the beholder; and with one foot
slightly advanced she seemed in the act of step-

ping forward to bestow a kiss. And a brazen tablet let into the black marble of the pedestal bore, in five learned tongues, the strange inscription: —

"Created by the hand of one maddened by love, I madden all who gaze upon me. Mortal, condemned to live in solitude with me, prepare thyself to die of love at my feet. The old gods, worshiped by youth and beauty, are dead; and no immortal power can place a living heart in this stony bosom or lend to these matchless limbs the warm flexibility and rosiness of life."

*

* *

Around the chamber of the statue ran a marble wainscoting chiseled with Bacchanal bas-reliefs — a revel of rude dryads and fauns linking themselves in amorous interlacings; — upon an altar of porphyry flickered the low flame of the holy fire fed with leaves of the myrtle sacred to love; — doves for the sacrifice were cooing and wooing in the marble court without; — a sound of crystal water came from a fountain near the threshold, where beautiful feminine monsters, whose lithe flanks blended into serpent coils,

upheld in their arms of bronze the fantastic cup
from which the living waters leapt; a balmy,
sensuous air, bearing on its wings the ghosts of
perfumes known to the voluptuaries of Corinth,
filled the softly lighted sanctuary; — and on
either side of the threshold stood two statues,
respectively in white and black marble —
Love, the blond brother of Death; Death, the
dark brother of Love, with torch forever extinguished.

And the King knew that the Prisoner kept
alive the sacred fire, and poured out the blood of
the doves at the feet of the goddess, who smiled
with the eternal smile of immortal youth and
changeless loveliness and the consciousness of the
mighty witchery of her enchanting body. For
secret watchers came to the palace and said: —

"When he first beheld the awful holiness of
her beauty, he fell prostrate as one bereft of
life, and long so remained."

And the King musingly made answer: —

"Aphrodite is no longer to be appeased with
the blood of doves, but only with the blood of
men — men of mighty hearts and volcanic
passion. He is youthful and strong and an artist! — and he must soon die. Let the weapons

of death be mercifully placed at the feet of
Aphrodite, that her victim may be able to offer
himself up in sacrifice."

*
*   *

Now the secret messengers were eunuchs.
And they came again to the palace, and whispered in the ears of the silver-bearded King:—

"He has again poured out the blood of the
doves, and he sings the sacred Hymn of Homer,
and kisses her marble body until his lips bleed;
— and the goddess still smiles the smile of
perfect loveliness that is pitiless."

And the King answered: —

"It is even as I desire."

A second time the messengers came to the
palace, and whispered in the ears of the iron-
eyed King: —

"He bathes her feet with his tears: his heart
is tortured as though crushed by fingers of marble; he no longer eats or slumbers, neither
drinks he the waters of the Fountain of Bronze;
— and the goddess still smiles the mocking
smile of eternal and perfect loveliness that is
without pity and without mercy."

107

FANTASTICS

And the King answered: —
"It is even as I had wished."

*

*   *

So one morning, in the first rosy flush of sunrise, they found the Prisoner dead, his arms
madly flung about the limbs of the goddess in a
last embrace, and his cheek resting upon her
marble foot. All the blood of his heart, gushing
from a wound in his breast, had been poured out
upon the pedestal of black marble; and it trick-
led down over the brazen tablet inscribed
with five ancient tongues, and over the mosaic
pavement, and over the marble threshold past
the statue of Love who is the brother of Death,
and the statue of Death who is the brother of
Love, until it mingled with the waters of the
Fountain of Bronze from which the sacrificial
doves did drink.

And around the bodies of the serpent-women
the waters blushed rosily; and above the dead,
the goddess still smiled the sweet and mocking
smile of eternal and perfect loveliness that hath
no pity.

"Thrice seven days he has lived at her feet,"

muttered the King; "yet even I, hoary with years, dare not trust myself to look upon her for an hour!" And a phantom of remorse, like a shadow from Erebus, passed across his face of granite. "Let her be broken in pieces," he said, "even as a vessel of glass is broken."

But the King's servants, beholding the white witchery of her rhythmic limbs, fell upon their faces; and there was no man found to raise his hand against the Medusa of beauty whose loveliness withered men's hearts as leaves are crisped by fire. And Aphrodite smiled down upon them with the smile of everlasting youth and immortal beauty and eternal mockery of human passion.

THE FOUNTAIN OF GOLD [1]

(THIS is the tale told in the last hours of a summer night to the old Spanish priest in the Hôtel Dieu, by an aged wanderer from the Spanish Americas; and I write it almost as I heard it from the priest's lips.)

"I could not sleep. The strange odors of the flowers; the sense of romantic excitement which fills a vivid imagination in a new land; the sight of a new heaven illuminated by unfamiliar constellations, and a new world which seemed to me a very garden of Eden, — perhaps all of these added to beget the spirit of unrest which consumed me as with a fever. I rose and went out under the stars. I heard the heavy breathing of the soldiers, whose steel corselets glimmered in the ghostly light; — the occasional snorting of the horses; — the regular tread of the sentries guarding the sleep of their comrades. An inexplicable longing came upon me to wander alone into the deep forest beyond, such a longing as in summer days in Seville had seized me when

[1] *Item*, October 15, 1880.

110

THE FOUNTAIN OF GOLD

I heard the bearded soldiers tell of the enchantment of the New World. I did not dream of danger; for in those days I feared neither God nor devil, and the Commander held me the most desperate of that desperate band of men. I strode out beyond the lines; — the grizzled sentry growled out a rough protest as I received his greeting in sullen silence; — I cursed him and passed on.

.   .   .   .

"The deep sapphire of that marvelous Southern night paled to pale amethyst; then the horizon brightened into yellow behind the crests of the palm trees; and at last the diamond-fires of the Southern Cross faded out. Far behind me I heard the Spanish bugles, ringing their call through the odorous air of that tropical morning, quaveringly sweet in the distance, faint as music from another world. Yet I did not dream of retracing my steps. As in a dream I wandered on under the same strange impulse, and the bugle-call again rang out, but fainter than before. I do not know if it was the strange perfume of the strange flowers, or the odors of the spice-bearing trees, or the caressing warmth of the tropical air, or witchcraft; but a new

sense of feeling came to me. I would have given
worlds to have been able to weep: I felt the
old fierceness die out of my heart; — wild doves
flew down from the trees and perched upon my
shoulders, and I laughed to find myself caressing them — I whose hands were red with
blood, and whose heart was black with crime.

.   .   .   .

"And the day broadened and brightened into
a paradise of emerald and gold; birds no larger
than bees, but painted with strange metallic
fires of color, hummed about me; — parrots
chattered in the trees; — apes swung themselves with fantastic agility from branch to
branch; — a million million blossoms of inexpressible beauty opened their silky hearts to
the sun; — and the drowsy perfume of the
dreamy woods became more intoxicating. It
seemed to me a land of witchcraft, such as the
Moors told us of in Spain, when they spoke of
countries lying near the rising of the sun. And
it came to pass that I found myself dreaming of
the Fountain of Gold which Ponce de Leon
sought.

.   .   .   .

"Then it seemed to me that the trees became loftier. The palms looked older than the deluge, and their cacique-plumes seemed to touch the azure of heaven. And suddenly I found myself within a great clear space, ringed in by the primeval trees so lofty that all within their circle was bathed in verdant shadow. The ground was carpeted with moss and odorous herbs and flowers, so thickly growing that the foot made no sound upon their elastic leaves and petals; and from the circle of the trees on every side the land sloped down to a vast basin filled with sparkling water, and there was a lofty jet in the midst of the basin, such as I had seen in the Moorish courts of Granada. The water was deep and clear as the eyes of a woman in her first hours of love; — I saw gold-sprinkled sands far below, and rainbow lights where the rain of the fountain made ripples. It seemed strange to me that the jet leaped from nothing formed by the hand of man; it was as though a mighty underflow forced it upward in a gush above the bright level of the basin. I unbuckled my armor and doffed my clothing, and plunged into the fountain with delight. It was far deeper than I expected; the crystalline purity of the water had deceived me — I could

not even dive to the bottom. I swam over to
the fountain jet and found to my astonishment
that while the waters of the basin were cool
as the flow of a mountain spring, the leaping
column of living crystal in its centre was warm
as blood!

. . . .

"I felt an inexpressible exhilaration from
my strange bath; I gamboled in the water like
a boy; I even cried aloud to the woods and the
birds; and the parrots shouted back my cries
from the heights of the palms. And, leaving
the fountain, I felt no fatigue or hunger; but
when I lay down a deep and leaden sleep came
upon me, — such a sleep as a child sleeps in the
arms of its mother.

. . . .

"When I awoke a woman was bending over
me. She was wholly unclad, and with her perfect beauty, and the tropical tint of her skin,
she looked like a statue of amber. Her flowing
black hair was interwoven with white flowers;
her eyes were very large, and dark and deep,
and fringed with silky lashes. She wore no ornaments of gold, like the Indian girls I had seen,
— only the white flowers in her hair. I looked

at her wonderingly as upon an angel; and with
her tall and slender grace she seemed to me,
indeed, of another world. For the first time in
all that dark life of mine, I felt fear in the presence of a woman; but a fear not unmixed with
pleasure. I spoke to her in Spanish; but she
only opened her dark eyes more widely, and
smiled. I made signs; she brought me fruits
and clear water in a gourd; and as she bent over
me again, I kissed her.

.   .   .   .

"Why should I tell of our love, Padre? —
let me only say that those were the happiest
years of my life. Earth and heaven seemed to
have embraced in that strange land; it was
Eden; it was paradise; never-wearying love,
eternal youth! No other mortal ever knew such
happiness as I; — yet none ever suffered so
agonizing a loss. We lived upon fruits and the
water of the Fountain; — our bed was the
moss and the flowers; the doves were our play-
mates; — the stars our lamps. Never storm or
cloud; — never rain or heat; — only the tepid
summer drowsy with sweet odors, the songs of
birds and murmuring water; the waving palms,
the jewel-breasted minstrels of the woods who

chanted to us through the night. And we never left the little valley. My armor and my good rapier rusted away; my garments were soon worn out; but there we needed no raiment, it was all warmth and light and repose. 'We shall never grow old here,' she whispered. But when I asked her if that was, indeed, the Fountain of Youth, she only smiled and placed her finger upon her lips. Neither could I ever learn her name. I could not acquire her tongue; yet she had learned mine with marvelous quickness. We never had a quarrel; — I could never find heart to even frown upon her. She was all gentleness, playfulness, loveliness — but what do you care, Padre, to hear all these things?

·　·　·　·　·　·　·　·

"Did I say our happiness was perfect? No: there was one strange cause of anxiety which regularly troubled me. Each night, while lying in her arms, I heard the Spanish bugle-call, — far and faint and ghostly as a voice from the dead. It seemed like a melancholy voice calling to me. And whenever the sound floated to us, I felt that she trembled, and wound her arms faster about me, and she would weep until I kissed away her tears. And through all those

116

years I heard the bugle-call. Did I say years?
— nay, *centuries!* — for in that land one never
grows old; I heard it through centuries after all
my companions were dead."

(The priest crossed himself under the lamplight, and murmured a prayer. "Continue,
hijo mio," he said at last; "tell me all.")

"It was anger, Padre; I wished to see for myself where the sounds came from that tortured
my life. And I know not why she slept so deeply
that night. As I bent over to kiss her, she
moaned in her dreams, and I saw a crystal tear
glimmer on the dark fringe of her eyes — and
then that cursed bugle-call —"

The old man's voice failed a moment. He
gave a feeble cough, spat blood, and went
on: —

"I have little time to tell you more, Padre.
I never could find my way back again to the
valley. I lost her forever. When I wandered
out among men, they spoke another language
that I could not speak; and the world was
changed. When I met Spaniards at last, they

spoke a tongue unlike what I heard in my youth. I did not dare to tell my story. They would have confined me with madmen. I speak the Spanish of other centuries; and the men of my own nation mock my quaint ways. Had I lived much in this new world of yours, I should have been regarded as mad, for my thoughts and ways are not of to-day; but I have spent my life among the swamps of the tropics, with the python and the cayman, in the heart of untrodden forests and by the shores of rivers that have no names, and the ruins of dead Indian cities, — until my strength died and my hair became white in looking for her."

"My son," cried the old priest, "banish these evil thoughts. I have heard your story; and any, save a priest, would believe you mad. I believe all you have told me; — the legends of the Church contain much that is equally strange. You have been a great sinner in your youth; and God has punished you by making your sins the very instrument of your punishment. Yet has He not preserved you through the centuries that you might repent? Banish all thoughts of the demon who still tempts you in the shape of a woman; repent and commend your soul to God, that I may absolve you."

"Repent!" said the dying man, fixing upon the priest's face his great black eyes, which flamed up again as with the fierce fires of his youth; "repent, father? I cannot repent! I love her! — I love her! And if there be a life beyond death, I shall love her through all time and eternity: — more than my own soul I love her! — more than my hope of heaven! — more than my fear of death and hell!"

The priest fell on his knees, and, covering his face, prayed fervently. When he lifted his eyes again, the soul had passed away unabsolved; but there was such a smile upon the dead face that the priest wondered, and, forgetting the *Miserere* upon his lips, involuntarily muttered: "He hath found Her at last." And the east brightened; and touched by the magic of the rising sun, the mists above his rising formed themselves into a Fountain of Gold.

A DEAD LOVE [1]

HE knew no rest; for all his dreams were haunted by her; and when he sought love, she came as the dead come between the living. So that, weary of his life, he passed away at last in the fevered summer of a tropical city; dying with her name upon his lips. And his face was no more seen in the palm-shadowed streets; but the sun rose and sank as before.

And that vague phantom life, which sometimes lives and thinks in the tomb where the body moulders, lingered and thought within the narrow marble bed where they laid him with the pious hope, — *que en paz descansa!*

Yet so weary of his life had the wanderer been that he could not even find the repose of the dead. And while the body sank into dust the phantom man found no rest in the darkness, and thought to himself, "I am even too weary to rest!"

There was a fissure in the wall of the tomb. And through it, and through the meshes of the web that a spider had spun across it, the dead

[1] *Item*, October 21, 1880.

looked, and saw the summer sky blazing like
amethyst; the palms swaying in the breezes
from the sea; the flowers in the shadows of the
sepulchres; the opal fires of the horizon; the
birds that sang, and the river that rolled its
whispering waves between tall palms and vast-
leaved plants to the heaving emerald of the
Spanish Main. The voices of women and sounds
of argentine laughter and of footsteps and of
music, and of merriment, also came through
the fissure in the wall of the tomb; — sometimes also the noise of the swift feet of horses,
and afar off the drowsy murmur made by the
toiling heart of the city. So that the dead
wished to live again; seeing that there was no
rest in the tomb.

And the gold-born days died in golden fire;
— and the moon whitened nightly the face of
the earth; and the perfume of the summer
passed away like a breath of incense; — but
the dead in the sepulchre could not wholly
die.

The voices of life entered his resting-place;
the murmur of the world spoke to him in the
darkness; the winds of the sea called to him
through the crannies of the tomb. So that he

could not rest. And yet for the dead there is no consolation of tears!

The stars in their silent courses looked down through the crannies of the tomb and passed on; the birds sang above him and flew to other lands; the lizards ran noiselessly above his bed of stone and as noiselessly departed; the spider at last ceased to renew her web of magical silk; the years came and went as before, but for the dead there was no rest!

And it came to pass that after many tropical moons had waxed and waned, and the summer was come, with a presence sweet as a fair woman's, — making the drowsy air odorous about her, — that she whose name was uttered by his lips when the Shadow of Death fell upon him, came to that city of palms, and to the ancient place of burial, and even to the tomb that was nameless.

And he knew the whisper of her robes; and from the heart of the dead man a flower sprang and passed through the fissure in the wall of the tomb and blossomed before her and breathed out its soul in passionate sweetness.

But she, knowing it not, passed by; and the sound of her footsteps died away forever!

AT THE CEMETERY [1]

"COME with me," he said, "that you may see
the contrast between poverty and riches, between the great and the humble, even among
the ranks of the dead; — for verily it hath been
said that there are sermons in stones."

And I passed with him through the Egyptian
gates, and beyond the pylons into the Alley
of Cypresses; and he showed me the dwelling-
place of the rich in the City of Eternal Sleep, —
the ponderous tombs of carven marble, the
white angels that mourned in stone, the pale
symbols of the urns, and the names inscribed
upon tablets of granite in letters of gold. But
I said to him: "These things interest me not; —
these tombs are but traditions of the wealth
once owned by men who dwell now where riches
avail nothing and all rest together in the dust."

Then my friend laughed softly to himself,
and taking my hand led me to a shadowy place
where the trees bent under their drooping bur-
dens of gray moss, and made waving silhouettes against the catacombed walls which girdle

[1] *Item*, November 1, 1880. Hearn's own title.

the cemetery. There the dead were numbered and piled away thickly upon the marble shelves, like those documents which none may destroy but which few care to read — the Archives of our Necropolis. And he pointed to a marble tablet closing the aperture of one of the little compartments in the lowest range of the catacombs, almost level with the grass at our feet.

There was no inscription, no name, no wreath, no vase. But some hand had fashioned a tiny flower-bed in front of the tablet, — a little garden about twelve inches in width and depth, — and had hemmed it about with a border of pink-tinted seashells, and had covered the black mould over with white sand, through which the green leaves and buds of the baby plants sprouted up.

"Nothing but love could have created that," said my companion, as a shadow of tenderness passed over his face; — "and that sand has been brought here from a long distance, and from the shores of the sea."

Then I looked and remembered wastes that I had seen, where sand-waves shifted with a dry and rustling sound, where no life was and no leaf grew, where all was death and barrenness. And here were flowers blooming in the midst of sand! — the desert blossoming! — love living in the midst of death! And I saw the print of a hand, a child's hand, — the tiny fingers that had made this poor little garden and smoothed the sand over the roots of the flowers.

"There is no name upon the tomb," said the voice of the friend who stood beside me; "yet why should there be?"

Why, indeed? I answered. Why should the world know the sweet secret of that child's love? Why should unsympathetic eyes read the legend of that grief? Is it not enough that those who loved the dead man know his place of rest, and come hither to whisper to him in his dreamless sleep?

I said *he;* for somehow or other the sight of that little garden created a strange fancy in my mind, a fancy concerning the dead. The shells and the sand were not the same as those usually used in the cemeteries. They had been brought from a great distance — from the moaning shores of the Mexican Gulf.

So that visions of a phantom sea arose before me; and mystic ships rocking in their agony upon shadowy waves; — and dreams of wild coasts where the weed-grown skeletons of wrecks lie buried in the ribbed sand.

And I thought, — Perhaps this was a sailor and perhaps the loving ones who come at intervals to visit his place of rest waited and watched and wept for a ship that never came back.

But when the sea gave up its dead, they bore him to his native city, and laid him in this humble grave, and brought hither the sand that the waves had kissed, and the pink-eared shells within whose secret spirals the moan of ocean lingers forever.

And from time to time his child comes to plant a frail blossom, and smooth the sand with her tiny fingers, talking softly the while, — perhaps only to herself, — perhaps to that dead father who comes to her in dreams.

"AÏDA" [1]

To Thebes, the giant city of a hundred gates, the city walled up to heaven, come the tidings of war from the south. Dark Ethiopia has risen against Egypt, the power "shadowing with wings" has invaded the kingdom of the Pharaohs, to rescue from captivity the beautiful Aïda, daughter of Amonasro, monarch of Ethiopia. Aïda is the slave of the enchanting Amneris, daughter of Pharaoh. Radames, chief among the great captains of Egypt, is beloved by Amneris; but he has looked upon the beauty of the slave-maiden, and told her in secret the story of his love.

*

* *

And Radames, wandering through the vastness of Pharaoh's palace, dreams of Aïda, and longs for power. Visions of grandeur tower before him like the colossi of Osiris in the temple courts; hopes and fears agitate his soul, as varying winds from desert or sea bend the crests of the *dhoums* to the four points of heaven. In

[1] *Item*, January 17, 1881. Hearn's own title.

127

fancy he finds himself seated at the king's
right hand, clad with the robes of honor, and
wearing the ring of might; — second only to the
most powerful of the Pharaohs. He lifts Aïda
to share his greatness; he binds her brows with
gold, and restores her to the land of her people.
And even as he dreams, Ramphis, the deep-
voiced priest, draws nigh, bearing the tidings of
war and of battle-thunder rolling up from the
land "shadowing with wings," which is beyond
the river of Ethiopia. The priest has consulted
with the Veiled Goddess, — Isis, whose awful
face no man may see and live. And the Veiled
One has chosen the great captain who shall
lead the hosts of Egypt. "O happy man! —
would that it were I!" cries Radames. But the
priest utters not the name, and passes down the
avenue of mighty pillars, and out into the day
beyond.

*

* *

Amneris, the daughter of Pharaoh, speaks
words of love to Radames. His lips answer, but
his heart is cold. And the subtle mind of the
Egyptian maiden divines the fatal secret. Shall
she hate her slave?

AÏDA

The priests summon the people of Egypt together; the will of the goddess is made manifest
by the lips of Pharaoh himself. Radames shall
lead the hosts of Egypt against the dark armies
of Ethiopia. A roar of acclamation goes up to
heaven. Aïda fears and weeps; it is against
her beloved father, Amonasro, that her lover
must lead the armies of the Nile. Radames
is summoned to the mysterious halls of the
Temple of Phthah: — through infinitely extending rows of columns illumined by holy flames
he is led to the inner sanctuary itself. The
linen-mantled priest performs the measure of
their ancient and symbolic dance; the warriors
clad in consecrated armor; about his loins is
girt a sacred sword; and the vast temple re-
echoes through all its deeps of dimness the harmonies of the awful hymn to the Eternal Spirit
of Fire.

The ceremony is consummated.

The monarch proclaims tremendous war.
Thebes opens her hundred mouths of brass and
vomits forth her nations of armies. The land
shakes to the earthquake of the chariot-roll; —
numberless as ears of corn are the spear-blades

of bronze; — the jaws of Egypt have opened
to devour her enemies!

*
*   *

Aïda has confessed her love in agony; Amneris has falsely told her that her lover has
fallen in battle. And the daughter of Pharaoh
is strong and jealous.

*
*   *

As the white moon moves around the earth,
as the stars circle in Egypt's rainless heaven,
so circle the dancing-girls in voluptuous joy
before the king, — gauze-robed or clad only
with jeweled girdles; — their limbs, supple as
the serpents charmed by the serpent charmer,
curve to the music of harpers harping upon
fantastic harps. The earth quakes again; there
is a sound in the distance as when a mighty tide
approaches the land — a sound as of the thunder-chanting sea. The hosts of Egypt return.
The chariots roar through the hundred gates of
Thebes. Innumerable armies defile before the
granite terraces of the Palace. Radames comes
in the glory of his victory. Pharaoh descends

from his throne to embrace him. "Ask what
thou wilt, O Radames, even though it be the
half of my kingdom!"

And Radames asks for the life of his cap-
tives. Amonasro is among them; and Aïda,
beholding him, fears with an exceeding great
fear. Yet none but she knows Amonasro; for he
wears the garb of a soldier — none but she, and
Radames. The priests cry for blood. But the
king must keep his vow. The prisoners are set
free. And Radames must wed the tall and
comely Amneris, Pharaoh's only daughter.

*
* *

It is night over Egypt. To Ramphis, the
deep-voiced priest, tall Amneris must go. It is
the eve of her nuptials. She must pray to the
Veiled One, the mystic mother of love, to bless
her happy union. Within the temple burn the
holy lights; incense smoulders in the tripods of
brass; solemn hymns resound through the vast-
pillared sanctuary. Without, under the stars,
Aïda glides like a shadow to meet her lover.

*
* *

FANTASTICS

It is not her lover who comes. It is her father!
"Aïda," mutters the deep but tender voice of
Amonasro, "thou hast the daughter of Pharaoh in thy power! Radames loves thee! Wilt
thou see again the blessed land of thy birth?
— wilt thou inhale the balm of our forests? —
wilt thou gaze upon our valleys and behold our
temples of gold, and pray to the gods of thy
fathers? Then it will only be needful for thee
to learn what path the Egyptians will follow!
Our people have risen in arms again! Radames
loves thee! — he will tell thee all! What! dost
thou hesitate? Refuse! — and they who died
to free thee from captivity shall arise from the
black gulf to curse thee! Refuse! — and the
shade of thy mother will return from the tomb
to curse thee! Refuse! — and I, thy father,
shall disown thee and invoke upon thy head
my everlasting curse!"

*

*   *

Radames comes! Amonasro, hiding in the
shadow of the palms, hears all. Radames be-
trays his country to Aïda. "Save thyself! — fly
with me!" she whispers to her lover. "Leave
thy gods; we shall worship together in the tem-

ples of my country. The desert shall be our nuptial couch! — the silent stars the witness of our love. Let my black hair cover thee as a tent; — my eyes sustain thee; — my kisses console thee." And as she twines about him and he inhales the perfume of her lips and feels the beating of her heart, Radames forgets country and honor and faith and fame; and the fatal word is spoken. *Napata!* — Amonasro, from the shadows of the palm trees, shouts the word in triumph! There is a clash of brazen blades; Radames is seized by priests and soldiers: Amonasro and his daughter fly under cover of the night.

*
* *

Vainly tall Amneris intercedes with the deep-voiced priest. Ramphis has spoken the word: "He shall die!" Vainly do the priests call upon Radames to defend himself against their terrible accusations. His lips are silent. He must die the death of traitors. They sentence him to living burial under the foundations of the temple, under the feet of the granite gods.

*
* *

FANTASTICS

Under the feet of the deities they have made
the tomb of Radames — a chasm wrought in a
mountain of hewn granite. Above it the weird-
faced gods with beards of basalt have sat for a
thousand years. Their eyes of stone have beheld the courses of the stars change in heaven;
generations have worshiped at their feet of
granite. Rivers have changed their courses;
dynasties have passed away since first they
took their seats upon their thrones of mountain
rock, and placed their giant hands upon their
knees. Changeless as the granite hill from
whose womb they were delivered by hieratic
art, they watch over the face of Egypt, far-
gazing through the pillars of the temple into
the palm-shadowed valley beyond. Their will
is inexorable as the hard rock of which their
forms are wrought; their faces have neither
pity nor mercy, because they are the faces of
gods!

*
* *

The priests close up the tomb; they chant
their holy and awful hymn. Radames finds his
Aïda beside him. She had concealed herself in
the darkness that she might die in his arms.

AÏDA

The footsteps of the priests, the sacred hymn,
die away. Alone in the darkness above, at the
feet of the silent gods, there is a sound as of a
woman's weeping. It is Amneris, the daughter
of the king. Below in everlasting gloom the
lovers are united at once in love and death.
And Osiris, forever impassible, gazes into the
infinite night with tearless eyes of stone.

EL VÓMITO [1]

THE mother was a small and almost grotesque personage, with a somewhat mediæval face, oaken colored and long and full of Gothic angularity; only her eyes were young, full of vivacity and keen comprehension. The daughter was tall and slight and dark; a skin with the tint of Mexican gold; hair dead black and heavy with snaky ripples in it that made one think of Medusa; eyes large and of almost sinister brilliancy, heavily shadowed and steady as a falcon's; she had that lengthened grace of dancing figures on Greek vases, but on her face reigned the motionless beauty of bronze — never a smile or frown. The mother, a professed sorceress, who told the fortunes of veiled women by the light of a lamp burning before a skull, did not seem to me half so weird a creature as the daughter. The girl always made me think of Southey's witch, kept young by enchantment to charm Thalaba.

[1] *Item*, March 21, 1881.

*

*   *

EL VÓMITO

The house was a mysterious ruin: walls green with morbid vegetation of some fungous kind; humid rooms with rotting furniture of a luxurious and antiquated pattern; shrieking stairways; yielding and groaning floors; corridors forever dripping with a cold sweat; bats under the roof and rats under the floor; snails moving up and down by night in wakes of phosphorescent slime; broken shutters, shattered glass, lockless doors, mysterious icy draughts, and elfish noises. Outside there was a kind of savage garden, — torchon trees, vines bearing spotted and suspicious flowers, Spanish bayonets growing in broken urns, agaves, palmettoes, something that looked like green elephant's ears, a monstrous and ill-smelling species of lily with a phallic pistil, and many vegetable eccentricities I have never seen before. In a little stable-yard at the farther end were dyspeptic chickens, nostalgic ducks, and a most ancient and rheumatic horse, whose feet were always in water, and who made nightmare moanings through all the hours of darkness. There were also dogs that never barked and spectral cats that never had a kittenhood. Still the very ghastliness of the place had its

137

FANTASTICS

fantastic charm for me. I remained; the drowsy
Southern spring came to vitalize vines and
lend a Japanese monstrosity to the tropical
jungle under my balconied window. Unfamiliar and extraordinary odors floated up from
the spotted flowers; and the snails crawled
upstairs less frequently than before. Then a
fierce and fevered summer!

*
*   *

It was late in the night when I was summoned to the Cuban's bedside: — a night of
such stifling and motionless heat as precedes
a Gulf storm: the moon, magnified by the
vapors, wore a spectral nimbus; the horizon
pulsed with feverish lightnings. Its white
flicker made shadowy the lamp-flame in the
sick-room at intervals. I bade them close the
windows. "*El Vómito?*" — already delirious;
strange ravings; the fine dark face phantom-
shadowed by death; singular and unfamiliar
symptoms of pulsation and temperature; extraordinary mental disturbance. Could this
be *Vómito?* There was an odd odor in the
room — ghostly, faint, but sufficiently per-

ceptible to affect the memory: — I suddenly
remembered the balcony overhanging the African wildness of the garden, the strange vines
that clung with webbed feet to the ruined wall,
and the peculiar, heavy, sickly, somnolent
smell of the spotted blossoms! — And as I
leaned over the patient, I became aware of
another perfume in the room, a perfume that
impregnated the pillow, — the odor of a woman's hair, the incense of a woman's youth
mingling with the phantoms of the flowers,
as ambrosia with venom, life with death, a
breath from paradise with an exhalation from
hell. From the bloodless lips of the sufferer,
as from the mouth of one oppressed by some
hideous dream, escaped the name of the witch's
daughter. And suddenly the house shuddered
through all its framework, as if under the
weight of invisible blows: — a mighty shaking
of walls and windows — the storm knocking
at the door.

*
*   *

I found myself alone with her; the moans
of the dying could not be shut out; and the
storm knocked louder and more loudly, de-

manding entrance. "*It is not the fever*," I said. "I have lived in lands of tropical fever; your lips are even now humid with his kisses, and you have condemned him. My knowledge avails nothing against this infernal craft; but I know also that you must know the antidote which will baffle death; — this man shall not die! — I do not fear you! — I will denounce you! — He shall not die!"

For the first time I beheld her smile — the smile of secret strength that scorns opposition. Gleaming through the diaphanous whiteness of her loose robe, the lamplight wrought in silhouette the serpentine grace of her body like the figure of an Egyptian dancer in a mist of veils, and her splendid hair coiled about her like the viperine locks of a gorgon.

"*La voluntad de mi madre!*" she answered calmly. "You are too late! You shall not denounce us! Even could you do so, you could prove nothing. Your science, as you have said, is worth nothing here. Do you pity the fly that nourishes the spider? You shall do nothing so foolish, señor doctor, but you will certify that the stranger has died of the *vómito*. You do not know anything; you shall not know

EL VÓMITO

anything. You will be recompensed. We are rich." — Without, the knocking increased, as if the thunder sought to enter: I, within, looked upon her face, and the face was passionless and motionless as the face of a woman of bronze.

*
* *

She had not spoken, but I felt her serpent litheness wound about me, her heart beating against my breast, her arms tightening about my neck, the perfume of her hair and of her youth and of her breath intoxicating me as an exhalation of enchantment. I could not speak; I could not resist; spellbound by a mingling of fascination and pleasure, witchcraft and passion, weakness and fear — and the storm awfully knocked without, as if summoning the stranger; and his moaning ceased.

*
* *

Whence she came, the mother, I know not. She seemed to have risen from beneath: —

"The doctor is conscientious! — he cares for his patient well. The stranger will need his excellent attention no more. The conscientious doctor has accepted his recompense; he will certify what we desire, — will he not, *hija mia?*"

And the girl mocked me with her eyes, and laughed fiercely.

THE IDYL OF A FRENCH SNUFF–BOX[1]

THE old Creole gentleman had forgotten his snuff-box — the snuff-box he had carried constantly with him for thirty years, and which he had purchased in Paris in days when Louisiana planters traveled through Europe leaving a wake of gold behind them, the trail of a tropical sunset of wealth. It was lying upon my table. Decidedly the old gentleman's memory was failing!

There was a dream of Theocritus wrought upon the ivory lid of the snuff-box, created by a hand so cunning that its work had withstood unscathed all the accidents of thirty odd years of careless usage — a slumbering dryad; an amorous faun!

The dryad was sleeping like a bacchante weary of love and wine, half-lying upon her side; half upon her bosom, pillowing her charming head upon one arm. Her bed was a mossy knoll; its front transformed by artistic magic into one of those Renaissance scroll-

[1] *Item*, April 5, 1881.   Hearn's own title.

reliefs which are dreams of seashells; her ivory body moulded its nudity upon the curve of the knoll with antique grace.

Above her crouched the faun — a beautiful and mischievous faun. Lightly as a summer breeze, he lifted the robe she had flung over herself, and gazed upon her beauty. But around her polished thigh clung a loving snake, the guardian of her sleep; and the snake raised its jeweled head and fixed upon the faun its glittering topaz eyes.

There the graven narrative closed its chapter of ivory: forever provokingly motionless the lithe limbs of the dryad and the serpent thigh-bracelet and the unhappily amorous faun holding the drapery rigid in his outstretched hand.

*

* *

I fell asleep, still haunted by the unfinished idyl. The night filled the darkness with whispers and with dreams; and in a luminous cloud I beheld again the faun and the sleeping nymph and the serpent with topaz eyes coiled about her thigh.

Then the scene grew clear and large and

144

warm; the figures moved and lived. It was an Arcadian vale, myrtle-shadowed, and sweet with the breath of summer winds. The brooks purled in the distance; bird voices twittered in the rustling laurels; the sun's liquid gold filtered through the leafy network above; the flowers swung their fragile censers and sweetened all the place. I saw the smooth breast of the faun rise and fall with his passionate panting; I fancied I could see his heart beat. And the serpent stirred its jeweled head with the topaz eyes.

Then the faun moved his lips in sound — a sound like the cooing of a dove in the coming of summer, and an answering coo rippled out from the myrtle trees. And softly as a flake of snow, a white-bosomed thing with bright, gentle eyes alighted beside the faun, and cooed and cooed again, and drew yet a little farther off and cooed once more.

Then the serpent looked upon the dove — which is sacred to Aphrodite — and glided from its smooth resting-place, as water glides between the fingers of a hunter who drinks from the hollow of his hand in hours of torrid heat and weariness. And the dove, still retreating, drew after her the guardian snake with topaz eyes.

Then with all her body kissed by the summer breeze, the nymph awoke, and her opening eyes looked into the eager eyes of the faun; and she started not, neither did she seem afraid. And stretching herself upon the soft moss after the refreshment of slumber, she flung her rounded arms back, and linked them about the neck of the faun; and they kissed each other, and the doves cooed in the myrtles.

And from afar off came yet a sweeter sound than the caressing voices of the doves — a long ripple of gentle melody, rising and falling like the sighing of an amorous zephyr, melancholy yet pleasing like the melancholy of love — Pan playing upon his pipe! —

There was a sudden knocking at the door: —

"*Pardon, mon jeune ami; j'oubliais ma taba-tière! Ah! la voici! Je vous remercie!*" —

Alas! the vision never returned! The idyl remains a fragment! I cannot tell you what became of the dove and the serpent with topaz eyes.

SPRING PHANTOMS [1]

THE moon, descending her staircase of clouds in one of the "Petits Poèmes en Prose," enters the chamber of a newborn child, and whispers into his dreams: "Thou shalt love all that loves me, — the water that is formless and multiform, the vast green sea, the place where thou shalt never be, the woman thou shalt never know."

For those of us thus blessed or cursed at our birth, this is perhaps the special season of such dreams — of nostalgia, vague as the world-sickness, for the places where we shall never be; and fancies as delicate as arabesques of smoke concerning the woman we shall never know. There is a languor in the air; the winds sleep; the flowers exhale their souls in incense; near sounds seem distant, as if the sense of time and space were affected by hashish; the sunsets paint in the west pictures of phantom-gold, as of those islands at the mere aspect of whose beauty crews mutinied and burned their ships;

[1] *Item*, April 21, 1881. Hearn's own title.

147

plants that droop and cling assume a more feminine grace; and the minstrel of Southern woods mingles the sweet rippling of his mocking music with the moonlight.

There have been sailors who, flung by some kind storm-wave on the shore of a Pacific Eden, to be beloved for years by some woman dark but beautiful, subsequently returned by stealth to the turmoil of civilization and labor, and vainly regretted, in the dust and roar and sunlessness of daily toil, the abandoned paradise they could never see again. Is it not such a feeling as this that haunts the mind in springtime; — a faint nostalgic longing for the place where we shall never be; — a vision made even more fairylike by such a vague dream of glory as enchanted those Spanish souls who sought and never found El Dorado?

Each time the vision returns, is it not more enchanting than before, as a recurring dream of the night in which we behold places we can never see except through dream-haze, gilded by a phantom sun? It is sadder each time, this fancy; for it brings with it the memory of older apparitions, as of places visited in childhood, in that sweet dim time so long ago that its dreams and realities are mingled together in strange confusion, as clouds with waters.

Each year it comes to haunt us, like the vision of the Adelantado of the Seven Cities,— the place where we shall never be, — and each year there will be a weirder sweetness and a more fantastic glory about the vision. And perhaps in the hours of the last beating of the heart, before sinking into that abyss of changeless deeps above whose shadowless sleep no dreams move their impalpable wings, we shall see it once more, wrapped in strange luminosity, submerged in the orange radiance of a Pacific sunset, — the place where we shall never be!

And the Woman that we shall never know!

She is the daughter of mist and light, — a phantom bride who becomes visible to us only during those magic hours when the moon enchants the world; she is the most feminine of all sweetly feminine things, the most complaisant, the least capricious. Hers is the fascination of the succubus without the red thirst of the vampire. She always wears the garb that most pleases us — when she wears any; always adopts the aspect of beauty most charming to us — blond or swarthy, Greek or Egyptian,

Nubian or Circassian. She fills the place of a thousand odalisques, owns all the arts of the harem of Solomon: all the loveliness we love retrospectively, all the charms we worship in the present, are combined in her. She comes as the dead come, who never speak; yet without speech she gratifies our voiceless caprice. Sometimes we foolishly fancy that we discover in some real, warm womanly personality, a trait or feature like unto hers; but time soon unmasks our error. We shall never see her in the harsh world of realities; for she is the creation of our own hearts, wrought Pygmalionwise, but of material too unsubstantial for even the power of a god to animate. Only the dreams of Brahma himself take substantial form: these are worlds and men and all their works, which shall pass away like smoke when the preserver ceases his slumber of a myriad million years.

She becomes more beautiful as we grow older, — this phantom love, born of the mist of poor human dreams, — so fair and faultless that her invisible presence makes us less reconciled to the frailties and foibles of real life. Perhaps she too has faults; but she has no faults for us except that of unsubstantiality. Involuntarily

SPRING PHANTOMS

we acquire the unjust habit of judging real women by her spectral standard; and the real always suffer for the ideal. So that when the fancy of a home and children — smiling faces, comfort, and a woman's friendship, the idea of something real to love and be loved by — comes to the haunted man in hours of disgust with the world and weariness of its hollow mockeries, — the Woman that he shall never know stands before him like a ghost with sweet sad eyes of warning, — and he dare not!

A KISS FANTASTICAL [1]

CURVES of cheek and throat, and shadow of loose hair, — the dark flash of dark eyes under the silk of black lashes, — a passing vision light as a dream of summer, — the sweet temptations of seventeen years' grace, — womanhood at its springtime, when the bud is bursting through the blossom, — the patter of feet that hardly touch ground in their elastic movement, — the light loose dress, moulding its softness upon the limbs beneath it, betraying much, suggesting the rest; — an apparition seen only for a moment passing through the subdued light of a vineshaded window, briefly as an object illuminated by lightning, — yet such a moment may well be recorded by the guardian angels of men's lives.

*
* *

"*Croyez-vous ça ?*" suddenly demands a metallically sonorous voice at the other side of the table.

[1] *Item*, June 8, 1881. Hearn's own title.

A KISS FANTASTICAL

"Pardon! — qu'est ce que c'est?" asks the stranger, in the tone of one suddenly awakened, internally annoyed at being disturbed, yet anxious to appear deeply interested. They had been talking of Japan — and the traveler, suddenly regaining the clue of the conversation, spoke of a bath-house at Yokohama, and of strange things he had seen there, until the memory of the recent vision mingled fantastically with recollections of the Japanese bathing-house, and he sank into another reverie, leaving the untasted cup of black coffee before him to mingle its dying aroma with the odor of the cigarettes.

*
* *

For there are living apparitions that affect men more deeply than fancied visits from the world of ghosts; — numbing respiration momentarily, making the blood to gather about the heart like a great weight, hushing the voice to a murmur, creating an indescribable oppression in the throat, — until nature seeks relief in a strong sigh that fills the lungs with air again and cools for a brief moment the sudden fever of the veins. The vision may endure but an instant — seen under a gleam of sunshine, or through the antiquated gateway one passes from time to time on his way to the serious part of the city; yet that instant is enough to change the currents of the blood, and slacken the reins of the will, and make us deaf and blind and dumb for a time to the world of SOLID FACT. The whole being is momentarily absorbed, enslaved by a vague and voiceless desire to touch her, to kiss her, to bite her.

*
* *

The lemon-gold blaze in the west faded out; the blue became purple; and in the purple the mighty arch of stars burst into illumination, with its myriad blossoms of fire white as a woman's milk. A Spanish officer improved a momentary lull in the conversation by touching a guitar, and all eyes turned toward the musician, who suddenly wrung from his instrument the nervous, passionate, semi-barbaric melody of a Spanish dance. For a moment he played to an absolutely motionless audience; the very waving of the fans ceased, the listeners held their breath. Then two figures glided through the

154

A KISS FANTASTICAL

vine-framed doorway, and took their seats.
One was the Vision of a few hours before —
a type of semi-tropical grace, with the bloom of
Southern youth upon her dark skin. The other
immediately impressed the stranger as the ugli-
est little Mexican woman he had ever seen in
the course of a long and experienced life.

She was grotesque as a Chinese image of
Buddha, no taller than a child of ten, but very
broadly built. Her skin had the ochre tint of
new copper; her forehead was large and dis-
agreeably high; her nose flat; her cheek-bones
very broad and prominent; her eyes small,
deeply set, and gray as pearls; her mouth alone
small, passionate, and pouting, with rather
thick lips, relieved the coarseness of her face.
Although so compactly built, she had no aspect
of plumpness or fleshiness: — she had the physical air of one of those little Mexican fillies
which are all nerve and sinew. Both women
were in white; and the dress of the little Mexican was short enough to expose a very pretty
foot and well-turned ankle.

*
* *

Another beautiful woman would scarcely have diverted the stranger's attention from the belle of the party that night; but that Mexican was so infernally ugly, and so devilishly comical, that he could not remove his eyes from her grotesque little face. He could not help remarking that her smile was pleasing if not pretty, and her teeth white as porcelain; that there was a strong, good-natured originality about her face, and that her uncouthness was only apparent, as she was the most accomplished dancer in the room. Even the belle's movements seemed heavy compared with hers; she appeared to dance as lightly as the hummingbird moves from blossom to blossom. By and by he found to his astonishment that this strange creature could fascinate without beauty and grace, and play coquette without art; also that her voice had pretty bird tones in it; likewise that the Spanish captain was very much interested in her, and determined to monopolize her as much as possible for the rest of the evening. And the stranger felt oddly annoyed thereat; and sought to console himself by the reflection that she was the most fantastically ugly little creature he had seen in his whole life. But for some mysterious reason consolation refused to come. "Well, I am going back to Honduras to-morrow," he thought, — "and there thoughts of women will give me very little concern."

*

*　*

"I protest against this kissing," cried the roguish host in a loud voice, evidently referring to something that had just taken place in the embrasure of the farther window. "*On fait venir l'eau dans la bouche!* Monopoly is strictly prohibited. *Our* rights and feelings must be taken into just consideration." Frenzied applause followed. What difference did it make? — they were the world's Bohemians — here to-day, there to-morrow! — before another moonrise they would be scattered west and south; — the ladies ought to kiss them all for good luck.

*

*　*

So the kiss of farewell was given under the great gate, overhung by vine-tendrils drooping like a woman's hair love-loosened.

*

*　*

FANTASTICS

The beauty's lips shrank from the pressure of the stranger's; — it was a fruitless phantom sort of kiss. "*Y yo, señor,*" cried the little Mexican, standing on tiptoe as she threw her arms about his neck. Everybody laughed except the recipient of the embrace. He had received an electric shock of passion which left him voiceless and speechless, and it seemed to him that his heart had ceased to beat.

Those carmine-edged lips seemed to have a special life of their own as of the gymnotus — as if crimsoned by something more lava-warm than young veins: they pressed upon his mouth with the motion of something that at once bites and sucks blood irresistibly but softly, like the great bats which absorb the life of sleepers in tropical forests; — there was something moist and cool and supple indescribable in their clinging touch, as of beautiful snaky things which, however firmly clasped, slip through the hand with boneless strength; — they could not themselves be kissed because they mesmerized and mastered the mouth presented to them; — their touch for the instant paralyzed the blood, but only to fill its motionless currents with unquenchable fires as strange as of a tropical volcano, so that the heart strove to rise from its bed to meet them, and all the life of the man seemed to have risen to his throat only to strangle there in its effort at self-release. A feeble description, indeed; but how can such a kiss be described?

.   .   .   .

Six months later the stranger came back from Honduras, and deposited some small but heavy bags in the care of his old host. Then he called the old man aside, and talked long and earnestly and passionately, like one who makes a confession.

The landlord burst into a good-natured laugh, "*Ah la drôle! — la vilaine petite drôle!* So she made you crazy also. *Mon cher*, you are not the only one, *pardieu!* But the idea of returning here on account of one kiss, and then to be too late, after all! She is gone, my friend, gone. God knows where. Such women are birds of passage. You might seek the whole world and never find her; again, you might meet her when least expected. But you are too late. She married the *guitarrista*."

THE BIRD AND THE GIRL[1]

SUDDENLY, from the heart of the magnolia, came a ripple of liquid notes, a delirium of melody, wilder than the passion of the nightingale, more intoxicating than the sweetness of the night, — the mockingbird calling to its mate.

"*Ah, comme c'est coquet! — comme c'est doux!*" — murmured the girl who stood by the gateway of the perfumed garden, holding up her mouth to be kissed with the simple confidence of a child.

"Not so sweet to me as your voice," he murmured, with lips close to her lips, and eyes looking into the liquid jet that shone through the silk of her black lashes.

The little Creole laughed a gentle little laugh of pleasure. "Have you birds like that in the West?" she asked.

"In cages," he said. "But very few. I have seen five hundred dollars paid for a fine singer. I wish you were a little mockingbird!"

"Why?"

[1] *Item*, June 14, 1881.

"Because I could take you along with me to-morrow."

"And sell me for five hundred dol — ?" (A kiss smothered the mischievous question.)

"For shame!"

"Won't you remember this night when you hear them sing in the cages? — poor little prisoners!"

"But we have none where I am now going. It is all wild out there; rough wooden houses and rough men! — no pets — not even a cat!"

"Then what would you do with a little bird in such a place? they would all laugh at you — would n't they?"

"No; I don't think so. Rough men love little pets."

"Little pets!"

"Like you, yes — too well!"

"Too well?"

"I did not mean to say that."

"But you did say it."

"I do not know what I say when I am looking into your eyes."

"Flatterer!"

*
*   *

FANTASTICS

The music and perfume of those hours came back to him in fragments of dreams all through the long voyage; — in slumber broken by the intervals of rapid travel on river and rail; the crash of loading under the flickering yellow of pine-fires; the steam song of boats chanting welcome or warning; voices of mate and roustabout; the roar of railroad depots; the rumble of baggage in air heavy with the oily breath of perspiring locomotives; the demands of conductors; the announcement of stations; — and at last the heavy jolting of the Western stage over rugged roads where the soil had a faint pink flush, and great coarse yellow flowers were growing.

*
* *

So the days and weeks and months passed on; and the far Western village with its single glaring street of white sand, blazed under the summer sun. At intervals came the United States mail-courier, booted and spurred and armed to the teeth, bearing with him always one small satiny note, stamped with the postmark of New Orleans, and faintly perfumed as by the ghost of a magnolia.

THE BIRD AND THE GIRL

"Smells like a woman — that," the bronzed rider sometimes growled out as he delivered the delicate missive with an unusually pleasant flash in his great falcon eyes, — eyes made fiercely keen by watching the horizon cut by the fantastic outline of Indian graves, the spiral flight of savage smoke far off which signals danger, and the spiral flight of vultures which signals death.

One day he came without a letter for the engineer — "She's forgotten you this week, Cap," he said in answer to the interrogating look, and rode away through the belt of woods, redolent of resinous gums and down the winding ways to the plain, where the eyeless buffalo skulls glimmered under the sun. Thus he came and thus departed through the rosiness of many a Western sunset, and brought no smile to the expectant face: "She's forgotten you again, Cap."

* * *

And one tepid night (the 24th of August, 18—), from the spicy shadows of the woods there rang out a bird-voice with strange exotic tones: "Sweet, sweet, sweet!" — then cas-

163

cades of dashing silver melody! — then long, liquid, passionate calls! — then a deep, rich ripple of caressing mellow notes, as of love languor oppressed that seeks to laugh. Men rose and went out under the moon to listen. There was something at once terribly and tenderly familiar to at least One in those sounds.

"What in Christ's name is that?" whispered a miner, as the melody quivered far up the white street.

"It is a mockingbird," answered another who had lived in lands of palmetto and palm.

And as the engineer listened, there seemed to float to him the flower-odors of a sunnier land; — the Western hills faded as clouds fade out of the sky; and before him lay once more the fair streets of a far city, glimmering with the Mexican silver of Southern moonlight; — again he saw the rigging of masts making cobweb lines across the faces of stars and white steamers sleeping in ranks along the river's crescent-curve, and cottages vine-garlanded or banana-shadowed, and woods in their dreamy drapery of Spanish moss.

*
* *

THE BIRD AND THE GIRL

"Got something for you this time," said the
United States mail-carrier, riding in weeks
later with his bronzed face made lurid by the
sanguine glow of sunset. He did not say "Cap"
this time; neither did he smile. The envelope
was larger than usual. The handwriting was
the handwriting of a man. It contained only
these words: —

DEAR ——, Hortense is dead. It happened
very suddenly on the night of the 24th. Come
home at once.

S ——.

THE TALE OF A FAN [1]

PAH! it is too devilishly hot to write anything about anything practical and serious — let us dream dreams.

. . . .

We picked up a little fan in a street-car the other day, — a Japanese fabric, with bursts of blue sky upon it, and grotesque foliage sharply cut against a horizon of white paper; and wonderful clouds as pink as Love, and birds of form as unfamiliar as the extinct wonders of ornithology resurrected by Cuvieresque art. Where did those Japanese get their exquisite taste for color and tint-contrasts? — is their sky so divinely blue? — are their sunsets so virginally carnation? — are the breasts of their maidens and the milky peaks of their mountains so white?

But the fairy colors were less strongly suggestive than something impalpable, invisible, indescribable, yet voluptuously enchanting which clung to the fan spirit-wise, — a tender little scent, — a mischievous perfume, — a

[1] *Item*, July 1, 1881. Hearn's own title.

166

titillating, tantalizing aroma, — an odor inspirational as of the sacred gums whose incense intoxicates the priests of oracles. Did you ever lay your hand upon a pillow covered with the living supple silk of a woman's hair? Well, the intoxicating odor of that hair is something not to be forgotten: if we might try to imagine what the ambrosial odors of paradise are, we dare not compare them to anything else; — the odor of youth in its pliancy, flexibility, rounded softness, delicious coolness, dove-daintiness, delightful plasticity, — all that suggests slenderness graceful as a Venetian wineglass, and suppleness as downy-soft as the necks of swans.

.   .   .   .

Naturally that little aroma itself provoked fancies; — as we looked at the fan we could almost evoke the spirit of a hand and arm, of phantom ivory, the glimmer of a ghostly ring, the shimmer of spectral lace about the wrist; — but nothing more. Yet it seemed to us that even odors might be analyzed; that perhaps in some future age men might describe persons they had never seen by such individual aromas, just as in the Arabian tale one describes mi-

167

nutely a maimed camel and its burthen which
he has never beheld.

There are blond and brunette odors; — the
white rose is sweet, but the ruddy is sweeter;
the perfume of pallid flowers may be potent,
as that of the tuberose whose intensity sickens
with surfeit of pleasures, but the odors of
deeply tinted flowers are passionate and sa-
tiate not, quenching desire only to rekindle it.

There are human blossoms more delicious
than any rose's heart nestling in pink. There
is a sharp, tart, invigorating, penetrating,
tropical sweetness in brunette perfumes; blond
odors are either faint as those of a Chinese
yellow rose, or fiercely ravishing as that of
the white jessamine — so bewitching for the
moment, but which few can endure all night
in the sleeping-room, making the heart of the
sleeper faint.

*

* *

Now the odor of the fan was not a blond
odor: — it was sharply sweet as new mown
hay in autumn, keenly pleasant as a clear
breeze blowing over sea foam: — what were
frankincense and spikenard and cinnamon and

THE TALE OF A FAN

all the odors of the merchant compared with
it? — what could have been compared with it,
indeed, save the smell of the garments of the
young Shulamitess or the whispering robes of
the Queen of Sheba? And these were brunettes.

The strength of living perfumes evidences
the comparative intensity of the life exhaling
them. Strong sweet odors bespeak the vigor
of youth in blossom. Intensity of life in the
brunette is usually coincident with nervous
activity and slender elegance. — Young, slen-
derly graceful, with dark eyes and hair, skin
probably a Spanish olive! — did such an one
lose a little Japanese fan in car No. —— of the
C. C. R. R. during the slumberous heat of
Wednesday morning?

A LEGEND [1]

AND it came to pass in those days that a plague fell upon mankind, slaying only the males and sparing the females for some mysterious reason.

So that there was only one man left alive upon the face of the earth; and he was remarkably fair to behold and comely and vigorous as an elephant.

And feeling the difficulties of his position, the man fled away to the mountains, armed with a Winchester rifle, and lived among the wild beasts of the forest. . . .

And the women pursued after him and surrounded the mountain; and prevailed upon the man, with subtle arguments and pleasant words, that he should deliver himself up into their hands.

And they made a treaty with him, that he should be defended from ill-usage and protected from fury and guarded about night and day with a guard.

[1] *Item*, July 21, 1881.   Hearn's own title.

A LEGEND

And the guard was officered by women who were philosophers, and who cared for nothing in this world beyond that which is strictly scientific and matter of fact, so that they were above all the temptations of this world.

And the man was lodged in a palace, and nourished with all the dainties of the world, but was not suffered to go forth, or to show himself in the streets; forasmuch as he was guarded even as a queen bee is guarded in the hive.

Neither was he suffered to occupy his mind with grave questions or to read serious books or discourse of serious things or to peruse aught that had not been previously approved by the committee of scientific women.

For that which wearieth the brain affecteth the well-being of the body.

And all the day long he heard the pleasant plash of fountain waters and inhaled delicious perfumes, and the fairest women in the world stood before him under the supervision of the philosophers.

And a great army was organized to guard him; and great wars were fought with the women of other nations on his account, so that nine millions and more of strong young women were killed.

But he was not permitted to know any of these things, lest it might trouble his mind; nor was he suffered to hear or behold aught that can be unpleasant to mortal ears. He was permitted only to gaze upon beautiful things — beautiful flowers and fair women, and matchless statues and marvelous pictures, and graven gems and magical vases, and cunningly devised work of goldsmiths and silversmiths. He was only suffered the music created by the fingers of the greatest musicians and by the throats of the most bewitching of singers.

And once a year out of every ten thousand women in the world the fairest one and the most complete in all things was chosen; and of those chosen ones the fairest and most perfect were again chosen; and out of these again the committee of philosophers selected one thousand; and out of these thousand the man chose three hundred.

For he was the only man in the whole world; and the committee of philosophers ordained that he should be permitted to remain en-

A LEGEND

tirely alone for sixty-five days in the year, lest
he might be, as it were, talked to death.

At first the man fell occasionally in love and
felt unhappy; but as the committee of philosophers always sent unto him women more beautiful and more adorable than any he had seen
before, he soon became reconciled to his lot.

And instead of committing the folly of loving
one woman in particular, he learned to love all
women in general.

And during fifty years he lived such a life
as even the angels might envy.

And before he died he had 15,273 children,
and 91,638 grandchildren.

And the children were brought up by the
nation, and permitted to do nothing except to
perfect their minds and bodies.

And in the third generation the descendants
of the man had increased even to two millions
of males, not including females, who were indeed few, so great was the universal desire for
males.

And in the tenth generation there were even
as many males as females.

And the world was regenerated.

THE GIPSY'S STORY [1]

THE summer's day had been buried in Charlemagne splendors of purple and gold; the Spanish sable of the night glittered with its jewel-belt of stars. The young moon had not yet lifted the silver horns of her Moslem standard in the far east. We were sailing over lukewarm waves, rising and falling softly as the breast of a sleeper; winds from the south bore to us a drowsy perfume of lemon-blossoms; and the yellow lights among the citron trees seemed, as we rocked upon the long swell, like the stars of Joseph's dream doing obeisance. Far beyond them a giant pharos glared at us with its single Cyclopean eye of bloodshot fire, dyeing the face of the pilot crimson as a pomegranate. At intervals the sea amorously lipped the smooth flanks of the vessel with a sharp sound; and ghostly fires played about our prow. Seated upon a coil of rope a *guitarrista* sang, improvising as he sang, one of those sweetly monotonous ballads which the Andalusian gypsies term *soleariyas*. Even now the

[1] *Item*, August 18, 1881.

174

rich tones of that solitary voice vibrate in our
memory, almost as on that perfumed sea, under
the light of summer stars: —

> Sera,
> Para mi er mayo delirio
> Berte y no poerte habla.
> Gacho,
> Gacho que no hab ya motas
> Es un barco sin timon.
> Por ti,
> Las horitas e la noche
> Me las paso sin dormi.
> Sereno,
> No de oste la boz tan arta
> Que quieo dormi y no pueo.
> Marina,
> Con que te lavas la cara
> Que la tienes tan dibina?

Why he told me his story I know not: I
know only that our hearts understood each
other.

*

* *

"Of my mother," he said, "I knew little
when a child; I only remember her in memories
vague as dreams, and perhaps in dreams also.
For there are years of our childhood so mingled
with dreams that we cannot discern through
memory the shadow from the substance. But

in those times I was forever haunted by a voice that spoke a tongue only familiar to me in after years, and by a face I do not ever remember to have kissed.

"A clear, dark face, strong and delicate, with sharp crescent brows and singularly large eyes, liquidly black, bending over me in my sleep — the face of a tall woman. There was something savage even in the tenderness of the great luminous eyes, — such a look as the hunter finds in the eyes of fierce birds when he climbs to their nests above the clouds; and this dark dream-face filled me with strange love and fear. The hair, flowing back from her temples in long ripples of jet, was confined by a broad silver comb curved and gleaming like a new moon.

"And at last when these dreams came upon me, and the half-fierce, loving eyes looked upon me in the night, I would awake and go out under the stars and sob.

"A vast unrest possessed me; a new heat throbbed in my veins, and I heard forever flute-tones of a strange voice, speaking in an unknown tongue; — but far, far off, like the sounds of words broken and borne away in fragments by some wandering wind.

THE GIPSY'S STORY

"Ocean breezes sang in my ears the song of waves, — of waves chanting the deep hymn that no musician can learn, — the mystic hymn whereof no human ear may ever discern the words, — the magical hymn that is older than the world, and weirder than the moon.

"The winds of the woods bore me odors of tears of spicy gums and the sounds of bird-voices sweeter than the plaint of running water, and whispers of shaking shadows, and the refrain of that mighty harp-song which the pines sing, and the vaporous souls of flowers, and the mysteries of succubus-vines that strangle the oaks with love.

"Winds also, piercing and cold as Northern eyes, came to me from the abysses of the rocks, and from peaks whose ermine of snow has never since the being of the world felt the pressure of a bird's foot; and they sang Runic chants of mountain freedom, where the lightnings cross their flickerings. And with these winds came also shadows of birds, far circling above me, with eyes fierce and beautiful as the eyes of my dream.

*
* *

FANTASTICS

"So that a great envy came upon me of the winds and waves and birds that circle forever with the eternal circling of the world. Nightly the large eyes, half fierce, half tender, glimmered through my sleep: — phantom winds called to me, and shadowy seas chanted through their foam-flecked lips runes weird as the Runes of Odin.

*
*　　*

"And I hated cities with the hatred of the camel, — the camel that sobs and moans on beholding afar, on the yellow rim of the desert, the corpse-white finger of a minaret pointing to the dome of Mahomet's heaven.

"Also I hated the rumble of traffic and the roar of the race for gold; the shadows of palaces on burning streets; the sound of toiling feet; the black breath of towered chimneys; and the vast machines, forever laboring with sinews of brass, and panting with heart of steam and steel.

"Only loved I the eyes of night and the women eyes that haunted me, — the silence of rolling plains, the whispers of untrodden woods, the shadows of flying birds and fleet-

ing clouds, the heaving emerald of waves, the
silver lamentation of brooks, the thunder roll
of that mighty hymn of hexameters which the
ocean must eternally sing to the stars.

*
* *

"Once, and once only, did I speak to my
father of the dark and beautiful dream that
floated to me on the misty waves of sleep.
Once, and once only; for I beheld his face grow
whiter than the face of Death.

*
* *

"Encompassed about by wealth and pleasure, I still felt like a bird in a cage of gold.
Books I loved only because they taught me
mysteries of sky and sea — the alchemy of
suns, the magic of seasons, the marvels of
lands to which we long forever to sail, yet may
never see. But I loved wild rides by night, and
long wrestling with waves silver-kissed by the
moon, and the musky breath of woods, where
wild doves wandered from shadow to shadow,
cooing love. And the strange beauty of the

falcon face, that haunted me forever, chilled my heart to the sun-haired maidens who sought our home, fair like tall idols of ivory and gold.

"Often, in the first pinkness of dawn, I rose from a restless sleep to look upon a mirror; thirsting to find in my own eyes some dark kindred with the eyes of my dreams; and often I felt in my veins the blood of a strange race, not my father's.

"I saw birds flying to the perfumed South; I watched the sea gulls seeking warmer coasts; I cursed the hawks for their freedom, — I cursed the riches that were the price of my bondage to civilization, the pleasures that were the guerdon of my isolation among a people not my own.

— "'O that I were a cloud,' I cried, 'to drift forever with the hollow wind! — O that I were a wave to pass from ocean to ocean, and chant my freedom in foam upon the rocks of a thousand coasts! — O that I might live even as the eagle, who may look into the face of the everlasting sun!'

"So the summer of my life came upon me, with a madness of longing for freedom — a

freedom as of winds and waves and birds —
and a vague love for that unknown people
whose wild blood made fever in my veins, —
until one starless night I fled my home forever.

*
*　*

"I slumbered in the woods at last; the birds
were singing in the emerald shadows above
when I awoke. A tall girl, lithe as a palm,
swarthy as Egypt, was gazing upon me. My
heart almost ceased to beat. I beheld in the
wild beauty of her dark face as it were the
shadow of the face that had haunted me; and
in the midnight of her eyes the eyes of my
dream. Circles of thin gold were in her ears;
— her brown arms and feet were bare. She
smiled not; but, keeping her great wild eyes
fixed upon mine, addressed me in a strange
tongue. Strange as India — yet not all strange
to me; for at the sound of its savage syllables
dusky chambers of memory long unvisited
reopened their doors and revealed forgotten
things. The tongue was the tongue spoken to
me in dreams through all those restless years.
And she, perceiving that I understood, al-

though I spoke not, pointed to far tents beyond the trees, and ascending spirals of lazy smoke.

" 'Whithersoever we go, thou shalt also go.' she murmured. 'Thou art of our people; the blood that flows in thy veins is also mine. We have long waited and watched for thee, summer by summer, in those months when the great longing comes upon us all. For thy mother was of my people; and thou who hast sucked her breasts mayst not live with the pale children of another race. The heaven is our tent; the birds guide our footsteps south and north; the stars lead us to the east and west. My people have sought word of thee even while wandering in lands of sunrise. Our blood is stronger than wine; our kindred dearer than gold. Thou wilt leave riches, pleasures, honors, and the life of cities for thy heart's sake; and I will be thy sister.'

"And I, having kissed her, followed her to the tents of her people, — my people, — the world wanderers of the most ancient East."

THE ONE PILL–BOX [1]

LIKE Nebuchadnezzar's furnace, the sun
seemed to blaze with sevenfold heat; the sky
glowed like steel in the process of blistering; a
haze yellow as the radiance above a crucible
gilded the streets; the great plants swooned in
the garden— fainting flowers laid their heads on
the dry clay; the winds were dead; the Yellow
Plague filled the city with invisible exhalations
of death. A silence as of cemeteries weighed
down upon the place; commerce slept a wast-
ing slumber; the iron muscles and brazen
bones of wealth machinery relaxed, and lungs
of steel ceased their panting; the ships had
spread their white wings and flown; the wharves
were desolate; the cotton-presses ceased their
mighty mastication, and no longer uttered
their titanic sighs.

*
*   *

The English mill-master had remained at

[1] *Item*, October 12, 1881.

his post, with the obstinate courage of his race,
until stricken down. There was a sound in his
ears as of rushing waters; darkness before his
eyes: the whispering of the nurses, the orders
of the physicians, the tinkling of glasses and
spoons, the bubbling of medicine poured out,
the sound of doors softly opened and closed,
and of visits made on tiptoe, he no longer heard
or remembered. The last object his eyes had
rested upon was a tiny white-and-red pill-box,
lying on the little table beside the bed.

The past came to him in shadowy pictures
between dark intervals of half-conscious suffering — of such violent pain in thighs and
loins as he remembered to have felt long years
before after some frightful fall from a broken
scaffolding. The sound in his ears of rushing
water gradually sharpened into a keener sound
— like the hum of machinery, like the purring
of revolving saws, gnawing their meal of odorous wood with invisibly rapid teeth. Odors of
cypress and pine, walnut and oak, seemed to
float to his nostrils — with sounds of planing
and beveling, hammering and polishing, subdued laughter of workmen, loud orders, hurrying feet, and above all the sharp, trilling purr

of the hungry saws, and the shaking rumble of the hundred-handed engines.

*
*   *

He was again in the little office, fresh with odors of resinous woods — seated at the tall desk whose thin legs trembled with the palpitation of the engine's heart. It seemed to him there was a vast press of work to be done, — enormous efforts to be made, — intricate contracts to be unknotted, — huge estimates to be made out, — agonizing errors to be remedied, — frightful miscalculations to be corrected, — a world of anxious faces impatiently watching him. Figures and diagrams swam before his eyes, — plans of façades, — mathematical calculations for stairways, — difficult angles of roofs, — puzzling arrangements of corridors. The drawings seemed to vary their shape with fantastic spitefulness; squares lengthened into parallelograms and distorted themselves into rhomboids, — circles mockingly formed themselves into ciphers, — triangles became superimposed, like the necromantic six-pointed star. Then numerals

mingled with the drawings, — columns of
magical figures which could never be added up,
because they seemed to lengthen themselves
at will with serpent elasticity, — a mad procession of confused notes in addition and sub-
traction, in division and multiplication, danced
before him. And the world of anxious faces
watched yet more impatiently.

*

*   *

All was dark again; the merciless pain in
loins and thighs had returned with sharp consciousness of the fever, and the insufferable
heat and skull-splitting headache — heavy
blankets and miserable helplessness — and the
recollection of the very, very small pill-box
on the table. Then it seemed to him there were
other pill-boxes — three! nine! twenty-seven!
eighty-one! one hundred and sixty-two! one
hundred and sixty-two very small pill-boxes.

*

*   *

He seemed to be wandering in a cemetery,
under blazing sunlight and in a blinding glare

of whitewashed tombs, whose skeletons of
brick were left bare in leprous patches by the
falling away of the plastering. And, wandering,
he came to a deep wall, catacombed from base
to summit with the resting-places of ten thousand dead; and there was one empty place
— one black void — inscribed with a name
strangely like his own. And a great weariness
and faintness came upon him; and the pains,
returning, carried back his thoughts to the
warmth and dimness of the sick-room.

*

*   *

It seemed to him that this could not be
death — he was too weary even to die! But
they would put him into the hollow void in the
wall! — they might: he would not resist, he
felt no fear. He could rest there very well even
for a hundred years. He had a gimlet somewhere! — they would let him take it with him;
— he could bore a tiny little hole in the wall so
that a thread of sunlight would creep into his
resting-place every day, and he could hear the
voices of the world about him. Yet perhaps
he should never be able to leave that dark

damp place again! — It was very possible; seeing that he was so tired. And there was so much to be arranged first: there were estimates and plans and contracts; and nobody else could make them out; and everything would be left in such confusion! And perhaps he might not even be able to think in a little while; all the knowledge he had stored up would be lost; nobody could think much or say much after having been buried. And he thought again of the pill-boxes — one hundred and sixty-two very small pill-boxes. No; there were exactly three hundred and sixty-six! Perhaps that was because it was leap year.

*
* *

Everything must be arranged at once! — at once! The pill-boxes would do; he could breathe his thoughts into them and close them tightly — recollections of estimates, corrections of plans, directions to the stair-builders, understanding with contractors, orders to the lumber dealers, instructions to Texan and Mississippi agents, answers to anxious architects, messages to the senior partner, explana-

tions to the firm of X and W. Then it seemed
to him that each little box received its deposit
of memories, and became light as flame, buoy-
ant as a bubble; — rising in the air to float
halfway between floor and ceiling. A great
anxiety suddenly came upon him; — the windows were all open, and the opening of the door
might cause a current. All these little thoughts
would float away! — yet he could not rise to
lock the door! The boxes were all there, floating above him light as motes in a sunbeam: —
there were so many now that he could not
count them! If the nurse would only stay
away! . . . Then all became dark again — a
darkness as of solid ebony, heavy, crushing,
black, blank, universal. . . .

All lost! Brutally the door opened and
closed again with a cruel clap of thunder. . . .
Yellow lightnings played circling before his
eyes. . . . The pill-boxes were gone! But was
not that the face of the doctor, anxious and
kindly? The burning day was dead; the sick
man turned his eyes to the open windows, and
beheld the fathomless purple of the night, and
the milky blossoms of the stars. And he strove
to speak, but could not! The light of a shaded

lamp falling upon the table illuminated a tiny object, blood-scarlet by day, carmine under the saffron artificial light. *There was only one pill-box.*

A RIVER REVERIE[1]

An old Western river port, lying in a wrinkle
of the hills, — a sharp slope down to the yellow water, glowing under the sun like molten
bronze, — a broken hollow square of buildings
framing it in, whose basements had been made
green by the lipping of water during inunda-
tions periodical as the rising of the Nile, — a
cannonade-rumble of drays over the boulders,
and muffled-drum thumping of cotton bales,
— white signs black-lettered with names of
steamboat companies, and the green lattice-
work of saloon doors flanked by empty kegs,
—above, church spires cutting the blue, — below, on the slope, hogsheads, bales, drays, cases,
boxes, barrels, kegs, mules, wagons, policemen,
loungers, and roustabouts, whose apparel is
at once as picturesque, as ragged, and as colorless as the fronts of their favorite haunts on the
water-front. Westward the purple of softly-
rolling hills beyond the flood, through a diaphanous veil of golden haze, — a marshaled
array of white boats with arabesque lightness

[1] *Times-Democrat*, May 2, 1882.

of painted woodwork, and a long and irregular line of smoking chimneys. The scene never varied save with the varying tints of weather and season. Sometimes the hills were gray through an atmosphere of rain, — sometimes they vanished altogether in an autumn fog; but the port never changed. And in summer or spring, at the foot of the iron stairway leading up to a steamboat agency in the great middle building facing the river, there was a folding stool — which no one ever tried to steal — which even the most hardened wharf thieves respected, — and on that stool, at the same hour every day, a pleasant-faced old man with a very long white beard used to sit. If you asked anybody who it was, the invariable reply was: "Oh! that's old Captain ——; used to be in the New Orleans trade; — had to give up the river on account of rheumatism; — comes down every day to look at things."

Wonder whether the old captain still sits there of bright afternoons, to watch the returning steamers panting with their mighty run from the Far South, — or whether he has sailed away upon that other river, silent and colorless as winter's fog, to that vast and

A RIVER REVERIE

shadowy port where much ghostly freight is discharged from vessels that never return? He haunts us sometimes, — even as he must have been haunted by the ghosts of dead years.

When some great white boat came in, uttering its long, wild cry of joy after its giant race of eighteen hundred miles, to be reëchoed by the hundred voices of the rolling hills, — surely the old man must have dreamed upon his folding stool of marvelous nights upon the Mississippi, — nights filled with the perfume of orange blossoms under a milky palpitation of stars in amethystine sky, and witchery of tropical moonlight.

The romance of river-life is not like the romance of the sea, — that romance memory evokes for us in the midst of the city by the simple exhalations of an asphalt pavement under the sun, — divine saltiness, celestial freshness, the wild joy of wind-kissed waves, the hum of rigging and crackling of cordage, the rocking as of a mighty cradle. But it is perhaps sweeter. There is no perceptible motion of the river vessel; it is like the movement of a balloon, so steady that not we but the world only seems to move. Under the stars there seems to unroll its endlessness like an immeasurable ribbon of silver-purple. There is a noiseless ripple in it, as of watered silk. There is a heavy, sweet smell of nature, of luxuriant verdure; the feminine outlines of the hills, dotted with the chrome-yellow of window-lights, are blue-black; the vast arch of stars blossoms overhead; there is no sound but the colossal breathing of the laboring engines; the stream widens; the banks lessen; the heavens seem to grow deeper, the stars whiter, the blue bluer. Under the night it is all a blue world, as in a planet illuminated by a colored sun. The calls of the passing boats, sonorous as the music of vast silver trumpets, ring out clear but echoless; — there are no hills to give ghostly answer. Days are born in gold and die in rose-color; and the stream widens, widens, broadens toward the eternity of the sea under the eternity of the sky. We sail out of Northern frosts into Southern lukewarmness, into the luxuriant and somnolent smell of magnolias and lemon-blossoms, — the sugar-country exhales its incense of welcome. And the giant crescent of lights, the stream-song of joyous boats, the world of chimneys, the forests of spars, the burst of morning glory over New Orleans, viewed from the deck of a pilot-house. . . .

These may never be wholly forgotten; after the lapse of fifty years in some dusty and dreary inland city, an odor, an echo, a printed name may resurrect their recollection, fresh as one of those Gulf winds that leave sweet odors after them, like coquettish women, like Talmudic angels.

So that we beheld all these things yesterday and heard all these dead voices once more; saw the old Western port with its water-be-slimed warehouses, and the Kentucky hills beyond the river, and the old captain on his folding stool, gazing wistfully at the boats; so that we heard once more the steam whistles of vessels that have long ceased to be, or that, changed into floating wharves, rise and fall with the flood, like corpses.

And all because there came an illustrious visitor to us, who reminded us of all these things; having once himself turned the pilot's wheel, through weird starlight or magical moonshine, gray rain or ghostly fog, golden sun or purple light, — down the great river

from Northern frosts to tepid Southern winds,
— and up the mighty stream into the misty
North again.

To-day his name is a household word in the
English-speaking world; his thoughts have
been translated into other tongues; his written
wit creates mirth at once in Paris salons and
in New Zealand homes. Fortune has also extended to him her stairway of gold; and he
has hobnobbed much with the great ones of
the world. But there is still something of the
pilot's cheery manner in his greeting, and the
keenness of the pilot's glance in his eyes, and a
looking out and afar off, as of the man who of
old was wont to peer into the darkness of starless nights, with the care of a hundred lives
on his hands.

He has seen many strange cities since that
day, — sailed upon many seas, — studied many
peoples, — written many wonderful books.

Yet, now that he is in New Orleans again,
one cannot help wondering whether his heart
does not sometimes prompt him to go to the
river, like that old captain of the far North-
western port, to watch the white boats panting
at the wharves, and listen to their cries of wel-

A RIVER REVERIE

come or farewell, and dream of nights beautiful, silver-blue, and silent, — and the great
Southern moon peering into a pilot-house.

"HIS HEART IS OLD" [1]

Chrystoblepharos — *Elikoblepharos,* — eyelids
grace-kissed, — the eyes of Leucothea,— the
dreaming marble head of the Capitoline Mu-
seum, — the face of the girl-nurse of the wine-
god, with a spray of wine-leaves filleting her
sweet hair, — that inexpressible, inexplicable,
petrified dream of loveliness, which well en-
ables us to comprehend old monkish tales
regarding the infernal powers of enchantment
possessed by the antique statues of those gods
who Tertullian affirmed were demons. For in
howsoever thoughtless a mood one may be
when he first visits the archæological shrine in
which the holiness of antique beauty reposes,
the first glorious view of such a marble miracle
compels the heart to slacken its motion in the
awful wonder of that moment. One breathes
low, as in sacred fear lest the vision might dissolve into nothingness — as though the witchery might be broken were living breath to
touch with its warm moisture that wonderful
marble cheek. Vainly may you strive to solve

[1] *Times-Democrat,* May 7, 1882.

the secret of this magical art; the exquisite mystery is divine — human eye may never pierce it; one dare not laugh, dare not speak in its presence — that beauty imposes silence by its very sweetness; one may pray voicelessly, one does not smile in presence of the Superhuman. And when hours of mute marveling have passed, the wonder seems even newer than before. Shall we wonder that early Christian zealots should have dashed these miracles to pieces, maddened by the silent glamour of beauty that defied analysis and seemed, indeed, a creation of the Master-Magician himself?

And the Centauress, in cameo, kneeling to suckle her little one; — the supple nudity of exquisite *ephebi* turning in eternal dance about the circumference of wondrous vases; — gentle Psyche, butterfly-winged, weeping on a graven carnelian; — river-deities in relief eternally watching the noiseless flow of marble waves from urns that gurgle not; — joyous Tritons with knotty backs and seaweed twined among their locks; — luxurious symposia in sculpture, such as might have well suggested the Oriental fancy of petrified cities, with their innumerable

pleasure-seekers suddenly turned to stone; —
splendid processions of maidens to the shrine
of the Maiden-Goddess, and Bacchantes leading tame panthers in the escort of the Rosy
God: all these and countless other visions of
the dead Greek world still haunted me, as I
laid aside the beautiful and quaint volume of
archæological learning that inspired them —
bound in old fashion, and bearing the imprint
of a firm that had ceased to exist ere the close
of the French Revolution, — a Rococo Win-
kelmann. And still they circled about me,
with the last smoke-wreaths of the last evening pipe, on the moonlight balcony, among
the shadows.

*
* *

Then as I dreamed the beautiful dead world
seemed to live again, in a luminous haze, in
an Elysian glow. The processions of stone
awoke from their sleep of two thousand years,
and moved and chanted; — marble dreams
became lithe flesh; — the phantom Arcadia
was peopled with shapes of unclad beauty; —
I saw eyelids as of Leucothea palpitating under
the kisses of the Charities, — the incarnate

loveliness superhuman of a thousand godlike beings, known to us only by their shadows in stone; — and the efflorescent youth of that vanished nation, whose idols were Beauty and Joy, — who laughed much and never wept, — whose perfect faces were never clouded by the shadow of a grief, nor furrowed by the agony of thought, nor wrinkled by the bitterness of tears.

I found myself in the honeyed heart of that world, where all was youth and joy, — where the very air seemed to thrill with new happiness in a paradise newly created, — where innumerable flowers, of genera unknown in these later years, filled the valley with amorous odor of spring. But I sat among them with the thoughts of the Nineteenth Century, and the heart of the Nineteenth Century, and the garb of the Nineteenth Century, which is black as a garb of mourning for the dead. And they drew about me, seeing that I laughed not at all, nor smiled, nor spoke; and low-whispering to one another, they murmured with a silky murmur as of summer winds: —

"His heart is old!"

*
*　　*

FANTASTICS

And I pondered the words of the Ecclesiast: "Sorrow is better than laughter; for by the sadness of the countenance the heart is made better. . . . It is better to go to the house of mourning than to the house of feasting; and the day of one's death is better than the day of one's birth." But I answered nothing; and they spake again, whispering, "*His heart is old!*" And one with sweet and silky-lidded eyes, lifted her voice and spake: —

"O thou dreamer, wherefore evoke us, wherefore mourn us, — seeing that there is no more joy in the world?

"Ours was a world of light and of laughter and of flowers, of loveliness and of love. Thine is smoke-darkened and sombre; there is no beauty unveiled; and men have forgotten how to laugh.

"Ye have increased wisdom unto sorrow, and sorrow unto infinite despair; — for there is now no Elysium, — the vault of heaven has sunk back into immensity, and dissolved itself into nothingness; the boundaries of earth are set, and the earth itself resolved into a grain of dust, whirling in the vast white ring of innumerable suns and countless revolving worlds.

Yet we were happier, believing the blossoming of stars to be only drops of milk from the perfect breast of a goddess.

"Nymphs haunted our springs; dryads slumbered in the waving shadows of our trees; zephyrs ethereal rode upon our summer winds; and great Pan played upon his pipe in the emerald gloom of our summer woods. Ye men of to-day have analyzed all substances, decomposed all elements, to discover the Undiscoverable, and ye have found it not. But in searching for the unsearchable, ye have lost joy.

"We loved the beauty of youth, — the litheness of young limbs, — the rosy dawn of maturity, — the bloom of downy cheeks, — the sweetness of eyes sweetened by vague desires of life's spring, — the marvelous thrill of a first kiss, — the hunger of love which had only to announce itself to be appeased, — and the glory of strength. But ye have sought the secret of the Universal life in charnelhouses, — dismembering rottenness itself and prying open the jaws of Death to view the awful emptiness therein. Learning only enough to appal you, ye have found that science can teach you less of beauty than our forgotten gymnasiums; but in the mean time, ye have forgotten how to love.

"We gave to the bodies of our well-beloved the holy purification of fire; ye confide them to the flesh-eating earth, filling your cities with skeletons. For us Death was bodiless and terrible; for you she is visible and yet welcome; — for so weary have men become of life that her blackness seems to them beauty, — the beauty of a mistress, the universal Pasiphila, who alone can give consolation to hearts weary of life. So that ye have even forgotten how to die!

"And thou, O dreamer, thou knowest that there was no beginning and that there shall be no end; but thou dost also know that the dust beneath thy feet has lived and loved, that all which now lives once lived not, and that what is now lifeless will live again; — thou knowest that the substance of the sweetest lips has passed through myriad million transformations, that the light of the sweetest eyes will still pass through innumerable changes after the fires of the stars have burnt themselves out. In seeking the All-Soul, thou hast found it in thyself, and hast elevated thyself to deity, yet for thee are vows vain and oracles dumb. Hope is extinguished in everlasting night; thou mayst not claim even the consolation of prayer, for thou canst not pray to thyself. Like the Mephistopheles of thy poet, O dreamer of the Nineteenth Century, thou mayst sit between the Sphinx of the Past and the Sphinx of the Future, and question them, and open their lips of granite, and answer their mocking riddles. But thou mayst not forget how to weep, even though thy heart grow old." . . .

But I could not weep! — And the phantoms, marveling, murmured with a strange murmur. — " The heart of Medusa!"

MDCCCLIII [1]

SOMEBODY I knew was there, — a woman....

Heat, motionless and ponderous, as in some feverish colonial city rising from the venomous swamps of the Ivory Coast. The sky-blue seemed to bleach from the horizon's furnace edges, — even sounds were muffled and blunted by the heaviness of that air, — vaguely, as to a dozing brain, came the passing reverberation of footsteps; — the river-current was noiseless and thick and lazy, like wax-made fluid.... Such were the days, — and each day offered up a triple hecatomb to death, — and the faces of all the dead were yellow as flame....

Never a drop of rain: — the thin clouds which made themselves visible of evenings only, flocking about the dying fires of the west, seemed to dwellers in the city troops of ghosts departing with the day, as in the fantastic myths of the South Pacific.

... I passed the outer iron gate, — the warm sea-shells strewing the way broke under my feet with faint saline odors in the hot air:

[1] *Times-Democrat*, May 21, 1882. Hearn's own title.

MDCCCLIII

— I heard the iron tongue of a bell utter ONE, with the sinister vibration of a knell, — signaling the eternal extinction of a life. Seven and seventy times that iron tongue had uttered its grim monosyllable since the last setting of the sun. The grizzled watcher of the inner gate extended his pallid palm for that eleemosynary contribution exacted from all visitors; — and it seemed to me that I beheld the gray Ferryman of Shadows himself, silently awaiting his obolus from me, also a Shadow. And as I glided into the world of agony beyond, the dead-bell moved its iron tongue again — once. . . .

Vast bare gleaming corridors into which many doors exhaled odors of medicines and moans and sound of light footsteps hurrying — then I stood a moment all alone — a long moment that I repass sometimes in dreams. (Only that in dreams of the past there are no sounds — the dead are dumb; and the fondest may not retain the evanescent memory of a voice.) Then suddenly approached a swift step — so light, so light that it seemed the coming of a ghost; and I saw a slight figure black-robed from neck to feet, the fantastically winged cap of a Sister, and beneath the white cap a dark and beautiful face with very black eyes. Even then the iron bell spake again — once! I muttered — nay, I whispered, all fearful with the fearfulness of that place, the name of a ward and — the name of a Woman.

"Friend, friend! what do you want here?" murmured the Sister, who saw that the visitor was a stranger. Hers was the first voice I had heard in that place of death, and it seemed so sweet and clear, — a musical vibration of youth and hope! And I answered, this time audibly. "You are not afraid?" she asked. — "Come!"

Taking my hand, she led me thither — through spaces of sunlight and shadow, through broad and narrow ways, and between rows of beds white like rows of tombs. Her hand was cool and light as mist, — as frost, — as the guiding touch of that spirit might be whom the faithful of many creeds believe to lead their dead out of the darkness, into some vast new dawning beyond. . . . "You are not afraid? — not afraid?" the sweet voice asked again. And I suddenly became aware of the dead, lying between us, and the death-color in her face, like a flare of sunset. . . .

Then for an instant everything became dark between me and the Sister standing upon the other side of the dead — and I was groping in that darkness blindly, until I felt a cool hand grasp mine, leading me silently somewhere — somewhere into the light. "Come! you have no claim here, friend! you cannot take her back from God! — let us leave her with Him!" And I obeyed all voicelessly. I felt her light, cool hand leading me again between the long ranks of white beds, and through the vast, bare corridors, and the shining lobbies, and by the doors of a hundred chambers of death.

Then at the summit of the great stairway, she turned her rich gaze into my eyes with a strange, sweet, silent sympathy, pressed my hand an instant, and was gone. I heard the whisper of her departing robe; I saw the noiseless fluttering of her white cap; — a great door opened very silently, closed inaudibly; and I was all alone. — (Some one told me, only a few days later, that the iron bell had also spoken for her, the little Sister of Charity, — in the middle of the night, — once!)

FANTASTICS

And I, standing alone upon the stairs, felt something unutterably strange within me — the influence of that last look, perhaps still vibrating, like an expiring sunbeam, a dying tone. Something in her eyes had rekindled into life something long burned out within my heart — the ashes of a Faith entombed as in a sepulchral urn. . . . Yet only a moment; and the phantom flame sank back into its ashes; and I was in the sunlight again, iron of purpose as Pharaoh after the death of his firstborn. It was only a dead emotion, warmed to resurrection by the sunshine of a woman's eyes.

. . . Nevertheless, I fancy that when the Ringer is preparing to ring for me, — and the great darkness deepens all about me, — when sounds sink to their whispers and questions must remain eternally unanswered, — when memory is fading out into the infinite blackness, and those strange dreams that precurse the final dissolution marshal their illusions before me, — I fancy that I might hear again the whisper of a black robe, and feel a hand, light as frost, held out to me with the sweet questioning — *"Come! You are not afraid?"*

HIOUEN–THSANG [1]

The story of him who gave the Lotus of the good Law unto four hundred millions of his people in the Middle Kingdom, and remained insensible unto honors even as the rose-leaf to the dewdrop. . . .

Twelve hundred years ago, in a town of China, situated in the inmost recesses of the kingdom called Celestial, was born a boy, at whose advent in this world of illusions the spirits of good rejoiced, and marvelous things also happened — according to the legends of those years. For before his birth, the mother dreaming beheld the Shadow of Buddha above her, radiant as the face of the Mountain of Light; and after the Shadow had passed, she was aware of the figure of her son, that was to be, following after It over vast distances to cities of an architecture unknown, and through forests of strange growth that seemed not of this world. And a Voice gave her to know that her boy would yet travel in search of the Word through unknown lands, and be guided by Lord

[1] *Times-Democrat*, June 25, 1882. Hearn's own title.

Buddha in his wanderings, and find in the end
that which he sought. . . .

So the boy grew up in wisdom; and his face
became as the white face of the God in the
Temple beyond Tientsin, where the mirage
shifts its spectral beauties forever above the
sands, typifying to the faithful that the world
and all within it are but a phantasmagoria of
illusion. And the boy was instructed by the
priests of Buddha, and became wiser than they.

For the Law of Buddha had blossomed in
the land unnumbered years, and the Son of
Heaven had bowed down before it, and there
were in the Empire many thousand convents
of holy monks, and countless teachers of truth.
But in the lapse of a thousand years and more
the Lotus Flower of the Good Law had lost its
perfume; much of the wisdom of the World-
honored had been forgotten; fire and the fury
of persecution had made small the number of
holy books. When Hiouen-thsang sought for
the deeper wisdom of the Law he found it not;
nor was there in all China one who could inform
him. Then a great longing came upon him to
go to India, the land of the Savior of Man, and
there seek the wondrous words that had been

lost, and the marvelous books unread by Chinese eyes.

*

*   *

Before the time of Hiouen-thsang other Chinese pilgrims had visited the Indian Palestine; — Fabian had been sent thither upon a pilgrimage by a holy Empress. But these others had received aid of money and of servants, — letters to governors and gifts to kings. Hiouen-thsang had neither money nor servants, nor any knowledge of the way. Therefore he could only seek aid from the Emperor, and permission. But the Son of Heaven rejected the petition written upon yellow silk, and signed with two thousand devout names. Moreover, he forbade Hiouen-thsang to leave the kingdom under penalty of death.

But the heart of Hiouen-thsang told him that he must go. And he remembered that the caravans from India used to bring their strange wares to a city on the Hoang-ho — on the Yellow River. Secretly departing in the night, he traveled for many days, succored upon his way by the brethren, until he came to the caravansary, and saw the Indian merchants with their multitude of horses and of camels, resting beside the Hoang-ho.

And presently when they departed for the frontier, he followed secretly after them, with two Buddhist friends.

*
  *   *

So they came to the frontier, where the line of the fortifications stretched away lessening into the desert, with their watch-towers fantastically capped, like Mandarins. But here only the caravan could pass; for the guards had orders from the Son of Heaven to seize upon Hiouen-thsang; — and the Indian merchants rode away far beyond the line of the watch-towers; and the caravan became only a moving speck against the disk of the sun, to disappear with his setting. Yet in the night Hiouen-thsang passed with his friends, like shadows, through the line of guards, and followed the trail.

Happily the captain in charge of the next watch-tower was a holy man, and moved by the supplications of the Buddhist priests, he permitted Hiouen-thsang to pass on. But the other brethren trembled and returned, leaving Hiouen-thsang alone. Yet India was still more than a thousand miles distant, by the way of the caravans.

Only the men of the last watch-tower would not allow Hiouen-thsang to pass; but he escaped by them into the desert. Then he followed the line of the caravan, the prints of the feet of camels and horses leading toward India. Skeletons were whitening in the sands; the eyeless sockets of innumerable skulls looked at him. The sun set and rose again many times; the sand-sea moved its waves continually with a rustling sound; the multitude of white bones waxed vaster. And as Hiouen-thsang proceeded phantom cities mocked him on the right hand and upon the left, and the spectral caravans wrought by the mirage rode by him shadowlessly. Then his water-skin burst, and the desert drank up its contents; the hoof-prints disappeared. Hiouen-thsang had lost his way. . . .

*
*   *

From the past of twelve hundred years ago, we can hear the breaking of that water-skin;

— we can feel the voiceless despair that for a moment chilled the heart and faith of Hiouen-thsang, — alone in the desert of skeletons,— alone in the infinite platitude of sand broken only by the mockeries of the mirage. But the might of faith helped him on; prayers were his food, Buddha the star-compass that illuminated the path to India. For five days and five nights he traveled without meat or drink under blistering suns, under the vast throbbing of stars, — and at last the sharp yellow line of the horizon became green!

It was not the mirage, — it was a land of steel-bright lakes and long grass, — the land of the men who live upon horseback, — the country of the Oigour Tartars.

*
* *

The Khan received the pilgrim as a son; honors were showered upon him, — for the fame of Hiouen-thsang as a teacher of the Law had reached into the heart of Asia. And they desired that he should remain with them, to instruct them in the knowledge of Buddha. When he would not, — only after having vainly essayed upon him such temptation and coercion by turns that he was driven to despair, the Khan at last permitted him to depart under oath that he would return. But India was still far away. Hiouen-thsang had to pass through the territories of twenty-four great kings ere reaching the Himalayas. The Khan gave him an escort and letters to the rulers of all kingdoms, for his memory is yet blessed in the Empire Celestial.

It was in the seventh century. Rivers have changed their courses since then. Hiouenthsang visited the rulers of kingdoms that have utterly disappeared; he beheld civilizations where are now wastes of sand; he conversed with masters of a learning that has vanished without leaving a trace behind. The face of the world is changed; but the words of Hiouen-thsang change not; — lakes have dried up, yet we even now in this Western republic drink betimes from that Fountain of Gold which Hiouen-thsang set flowing — to flow forever!

So they beheld at last, afar off, the awful Himalayas, whose white turbans touch the heaven of India, vested with thunder-clouds, belted with lightnings! And Hiouen-thsang passed through gorges overhung by the drooping fangs of monsters of ice — through ravines so dark that the traveler beholds the stars above him at noonday, and eagles like dots against the sky — and hard by the icy cavern whence the sacred river leaps in roaring birth — and by winding ways to valleys eternally green — and ever thus into the glowing paradise of Hindustan. But of those that followed Hiouen-thsang, thirteen were buried in the eternal snow.

He saw the wondrous cities of India; he saw the sanctuaries of Benares; saw the great temples since destroyed for modern eyes by Moslem conquerors; saw the idols that had diamond eyes and bellies filled with food of emeralds and carbuncles; he trod where Buddha had walked; he came to Maghada, which is the Holy Land of India. Alone and on foot he traversed the jungles; the cobra hissed under his feet, the tiger glared at him with eyes that flamed like emeralds, the wild elephant's mountain-shadow fell across his path. Yet he feared nothing, for he sought Buddha. The Phansigars flung about his neck the noose of the

strangler, and yet loosened him on beholding
the holiness of his face; swarthy robbers, whose
mustaches were curved like scimitars, lifted
their blades to smite, and beholding his eyes
turned away. So he came to the Dragon-
Cavern of Purushapura to seek Buddha. For
Buddha, though having entered Nirvana a
thousand years, sometimes there made himself
visible as a luminous Shadow to those who
loved him.

*
* *

But in the cavern was a darkness as of the
grave, a silence as of death; Hiouen-thsang
prayed in vain, and vainly wept for many
hours in the darkness. At last there came a
faint glow upon the wall, like a beam of the
moon — and passed away. Then Hiouen-
thsang prayed yet more fervently than before;
and again in the darkness came a light — but a
fierce brightness as of lightning, as quickly
passing away. Yet a third time Hiouen-thsang
wept and prayed; and a white glory filled all
the black cavern — and brighter than the sun
against that glory appeared the figure and face
of Buddha, holier of beauty than all concep-

tions of man. So that Hiouen-thsang worshiped with his face to the earth. And Buddha
smiled upon him, making the heart of the pilgrim full of sunshine — but the Divine spoke
not, inasmuch as he had entered into Nirvana
a thousand years.

*

* *

After this Hiouen-thsang passed sixteen
years in the holy places, copying the Law, and
seeking the words of Buddha in books that had
been written in languages no longer spoken.
Of these he obtained one thousand three hundred and thirty-five volumes. Other volumes
there were in the Island of Elephants far to the
South — in sultry Ceylon; but thither it was
not permitted him to go.

He was a youth when he fled from China
into the desert; he was a gray man when he
returned. The Emperor that had forbade his
going now welcomed his return, with processions of tremendous splendor, in which were
borne the Golden Dragon and numberless
statues in gold. But Hiouen-thsang withdrew
from all honors into a monastery in the mountains, desiring to spend the rest of his life only

in translating the word of Buddha contained
in those many hundred books which he had
found. And of these before his death he
translated seven hundred and forty into one
thousand three hundred and thirty-five volumes, as the books of the Chinese are made.
Having completed his task, he passed away in
the midst of great sorrow; — the Empire wept
for him — four hundred millions mourned for
him.

*
* *

Did he see the Shadow of Buddha smile
upon him before he passed away, as he saw
it in the Dragon-Cavern at Purushapura? . . .
It is said that five others with him also beheld
that luminous presence in the cave. Yet we
may well believe that he only saw it — faith-
created; for Buddha having passed into Nirvana may be sought only in the hearts of men,
and seen only by the eyes of faith!

Twelve hundred years ago Hiouen-thsang
devoted his life to the pursuit of that he be-
lieved to be Truth, — abandoned all things for
what he held to be Duty, — encountered such
hardships as perhaps no other man ever en-

countered in the search for Wisdom. To-day nations that were unborn in his years are reaping the fruits of his grand sacrifice of self. His travels have been recently translated into the French tongue; his own translations are aiding the philologists of the nineteenth century to solve historical and ethnical problems; Max Müller lectures [1] upon his wonderful mission to India in the seventh century; and stories from the books he brought back from Maghada are in the hands of American readers. Who shall say that there is no goodness without the circle of Christianity! — who declare that heroism and unselfishness, and truth, and purest faith may not exist save within the small sphere of what we fancy the highest ethical civilization! The pilgrims to the Indian Palestine, the martyrs of the Indian Christ, are surely the brethren of all whom we honor in the history of self-abnegation and the good fight for truth.

[1] *Vide Chips from a German Workshop.*

L'AMOUR APRÈS LA MORT [1]

No rest he knew because of her. Even in the night his heart was ever startled from slumber as by the echo of her footfall; and dreams mocked him with tepid fancies of her lips; and when he sought forgetfulness in strange kisses her memory ever came shadowing between. . . . So that, weary of his life, he yielded it up at last in the fevered summer of a tropical city, — dying with her name upon his lips. And his face was no more seen in the palm-shadowed streets; — but the sun rose and sank even as before.

And that vague Something which lingers a little while within the tomb where the body moulders, lingered and dreamed within the long dark resting-place where they had laid him with the pious hope — *Que en paz descanse!*

Yet so weary of his life had the Wanderer been that the repose of the dead was not for

---

[1] *Times-Democrat*, April 6, 1884. Hearn's own title. Signed. Almost identical with the *Item* " Fantastic " of October 21, 1879.

him. And while the body shrank and sank into dust, the phantom man found no rest in the darkness, and thought dimly to himself: *"I am even too weary to find peace!"*

There was a thin crevice in the ancient wall of the tomb. And through it, and through the meshes of a web that a spider had woven athwart it, the dead looked and beheld the amethystine blaze of the summer sky, — and pliant palms bending in the warm wind, — and the opaline glow of the horizon, and fair pools bearing images of cypresses inverted, — and the birds that flitted from tomb to tomb and sang, — and flowers in the shadow of the sepulchres. . . . And the vast bright world seemed to him not so hateful as before.

Likewise the sounds of life assailed the faint senses of the dead through the thin crevice in the wall of the tomb: — always the far-off, drowsy murmur made by the toiling of the city's heart; sometimes sounds of passing converse and of steps, — echoes of music and of laughter, — chanting and chattering of children at play, — and the liquid babble of beautiful brown women.

. . . So that the dead man dreamed of life

and strength and joy, and the litheness of limbs
to be loved: also of that which had been, and
of that which might have been, and of that
which now could never be. And he longed at
last to live again — seeing that there was no
rest in the tomb.

But the gold-born days died in golden fire;
and blue nights unnumbered filled the land
with indigo-shadows; and the perfume of the
summer passed like a breath of incense — and
the dead within the sepulchre could not wholly
die.

Stars in their courses peered down through
the crevices of the tomb, and twinkled, and
passed on; winds of the sea shrieked to him
through the widening crannies of the tomb;
birds sang above him and flew to other lands;
the bright lizards that ran noiselessly over his
bed of stone, as noiselessly departed; the spider
at last ceased to repair her web of elfin silk;
years came and went with lentor inexpressible;
but for the dead there was no rest!

And after many tropical moons had waxed
and waned, and the summer was deepening in
the land, filling the golden air with tender
drowsiness and passional perfume, it strangely

FANTASTICS

came to pass that *She*, whose name had been
murmured by his lips when the Shadow of
Death fell upon him, came to that city of
palms, and even unto the ancient place of sep-
ulture, and unto the tomb that was nameless.

And he knew the whisper of her raiment —
knew the sweetness of her presence — and the
pallid hearts of the blossoms of a plant whose
blind roots had found food within the crevice
of the tomb, changed and flushed, and flamed
incarnadine. . . .

But She — perceiving it not — passed by;
and the sound of her footstep died away forever.

THE POST-OFFICE [1]

I

THE little steamer will bear you thither in
one summer day, — starting at early morning,
arriving just as the sun begins to rest his red
chin upon the edge of the west. It is a somewhat wearisome and a wonderfully tortuous
journey, through that same marshy labyrinth
by which the slavers in other days used to
smuggle their African freight up to the old
Creole city from the Gulf. . . . Leaving the
Mississippi by a lock-guarded opening in its
western levee, the miniature packet first enters
a long and narrow canal, — cutting straight
across plantations considerably below the level
of its raised banks, — and through this artificial waterway she struggles on, panting des-
perately under the scorching heat, until after
long hours she almost leaps, with a great steam-
sigh of relief, into the deeper and broader
bayou that serpentines through the swamp-

[1] *Times-Democrat*, October 19, 1884. Hearn's own
title. Signed.

forest. Then there is at least ample shadow;
the moss-hung trees fling their silhouettes right
across the water and into the woods on the
other side, morning and evening. Grotesque
roots — black, geniculated, gnarly — project
from the crumbling banks like bones from an
ancient grave; — dead, shrunken limbs and
fallen trunks lie macerating in the slime. Grim
shapes of cypress stoop above us, and seem to
point the way with anchylosed knobby finger,
— their squalid tatters of moss grazing our
smoke-stack. The banks swarm with crusta-
ceans, gnawing, burrowing, undermining; gray
saurians slumber among the gray floating logs
at the edge; gorged carrion-birds doze upon
the paralytic shoulders of cypresses, about
whose roots are coiled more serpents than ever
gnawed Yggdrasil. The silence is only broken
by the loud breathing of the little steamer; —
odors of vegetable death — smells of drowned
grasses and decomposing trunks and of eternal
mould-formation — make the air weighty to
breathe; and the green obscurities on either
hand deepen behind the crests of the water-
oaks and the bright masses of willow frondes-
cense. The parasitic life of the swamp, pendant

and enormous, gives the scene a drenched, half-drowned look, as of a land long-immersed, and pushed up again from profundities of stagnant water, — and still dripping with moisture and monstrous algæ. . . .

The ranks of the water-oaks become less serried,—the semitropical vegetation less puissant, — the willows and palmettoes and cypresses no longer bar out the horizon-light; and the bayou broadens into a shining, green-rimmed sheet of water, over which our little boat puffs a zigzag course, — feeling her way cautiously, — to enter a long chain of lakelets and lakes, all bayou-linked together. Sparser and lower becomes the foliage-line, lower also the banks; — the water-tints brighten bluely; the heavy and almost acrid odors of the swamp pass away. So thin the land is that from the little steamer's deck, as from a great altitude, the eye can range over immense distances. These are the skirts of the continent, trending in multitudinous tatters southward to the sea; — and the practiced gaze of the geologist can discern the history of prodigious alluvial formation, the slow creation of future prairie lands, in those long grassy tongues, — those

desolate islands, shaped like the letters of an
Oriental alphabet, — those reaches of flesh-
colored sand, that shift their shape with the
years, but never cease to grow.

Miles of sluggish, laboring travel, — sometimes over shallows of less than half a fathom,
— through archipelagoes whose islets become
more and more widely separated as we pro-
ceed. Then the water deepens steadily, —
and the sky also seems to deepen, — and there
is something in the bright air that makes
electrical commotion in the blood and fills the
lungs with richer life. Gulls with white breasts
and dark, broad wings sweep past with sharp,
plaintive cries; brown clouds of pelicans hover
above tiny islands within rifle-shot, — alter-
nately rising and descending all together.
Through luminous distances the eye can just
distinguish masses of foliage, madder-colored
by remoteness, that seem to float in suspension
between the brightness of the horizon and the
brightness of water, like shapes of the Fata
Morgana. And in those far, dim, island groves
prevails, perhaps, the strange belief that the
Universe itself is but a mirage; for the gods of
the most eastern East have been transported

thither, and the incense of Oriental prayer mounts thence into the azure of a Christian heaven. Those are Chinese fishing-stations, — miniature villages of palmetto huts, whose yellow populations still cling to the creed of Fo, — unless, indeed, they follow the more practical teachings of the Ancient Infant, born with snow-white hair, — the doctrine of the good Thai-chang-lao-kinn, the sublime Loo-tseu. . . .

II

Glassy-smooth the water sleeps along the northern coast of our island summer resort, as the boat slowly skirts the low beach, passing bright shallows where seines of stupendous extent are hung upon rows of high stakes to dry; — but already the ear is filled with a ponderous and powerful sound, rolling up from the south through groves of orange and lemon, — the sound of that "great voice that shakes the world." For less than half a mile away, — across the narrow island, — immense surges are whitening all the long slant of sand. . . . Divinely caressing the first far-off tones of that eternal voice to one revisiting ocean after absence of many weary and dusty summers, — tones filling the mind with even such vague blending of tenderness and of awe as the pious traveler might feel when, returning after long sojourn in a land of strange, grim gods, whose temple pavements may never be trodden by Occidental feet, he hears again the pacific harmonies of some cathedral organ, breaking all about him in waves of golden thunder.

. . . Then with a joyous shock we bump the ancient wooden wharf, — where groups of the brown island people are already waiting to scrutinize each new face with kindliest curiosity; for the advent of the mail-packet is ever a great and gladsome event. Even the dogs bark merry welcome, and run to be caressed. A tramway car receives the visitors, — baggage is piled on, — the driver clacks his tongue, — the mule starts, — the dogs rush on in advance to announce our coming.

III

In the autumn of the old feudal years, all this sea-girdled land was one quivering splendor of sugar-cane, walled in from besieging tides with impregnable miles of levee. But when the great decadence came, the rude sea gathered up its barbarian might, and beat down the strong dikes, and made waste the opulent soil, and, in Abimelech-fury, sowed the site of its conquests with salt. Some of the old buildings are left; — the sugar-house has been converted into an ample dining-hall; the former slave-quarters have been remodeled and fitted up for guests — a charming village of white cottages, shadowed by aged trees; the sugar-pans have been turned into water-vessels for the live stock; and the old plantation-bell, of honest metal and pure tone, now summons the visitor to each repast.

And all this little world, though sown with sand and salt, teems with extraordinary exuberance of life. Night and day the foliage of the long groves vibrates to chant of insect and feathered songster; and beyond reckoning are the varieties of nest-builders, — among whom very often may be perceived rose-colored or flame-colored strangers of the tropics, — flown hither over the Caribbean Sea. The waters are choked with fish; the horizon ever darkened with flights of birds; the very soil seems to stir, to creep, to breathe. Every little

bank, ditch, creek, swarms with "fiddlers,"
each holding high its single huge white claw
in readiness for battle; and the dryer lands are
haunted by myriads of ghostly crustacea, —
phantom crabs, — semi-diaphanous creatures
that flit over the land with the speed and lightness of tarantulas, and are so pale of shell that
their moving shadows first betray their presence. There are immense choruses of tree-frogs
by day, bamboulas of water-frogs after sundown. The vast vitality of the ocean seems to
interpenetrate all that sprouts, breathes, flies.
Cattle fatten wonderfully upon the tough wire-
grass; sheep multiply exceedingly. In every
chink something is trying to grow, in every
orifice some tiny life seeks to hide itself (even
beneath the edge of the table on which I wrote
some queer little creatures had built three marvelous nests of dry mud); — every substance
here appears not only to maintain life but to
create it; and ideas of spontaneous generation
present themselves with irresistible force.

IV

. . . And children in multitude! — children
of many races, and of many tints, — ranging

from ivorine to glossy bronze, through half
the shades of Broca's pattern-colors; — for
there is a strange blending of tribes and peoples here. By and by, when the youths and
maidens of these patriarchal families shall
mate, they will build for themselves funny
little timber-homes, — like those you see dot-
ting the furzy-green plain about the log-dwell-
ing of the oldest settler, — even as so many
dove-cots. Existence here is so facile, happy,
primitively simple, that trifles give joy un-
speakable; — in that bright air whose purity
defies the test of even the terrible solar microscope, neither misery nor malady may live.
To such contented minds surely the Past must
ever appear in a sunset-glow of gold; the Future
in eternal dawn of rose; — until, perchance,
the huge dim city summon some of them to her
dusty servitude, when the gray elders shall
have passed away, and the little patches of yel-
low-flowered meadow-land shall have changed
hands, and the island hath no more place for
all its children. . . . So they live and love, and
marry and give in marriage, and build their
little dove-cots, and pass away forever, —
either to smoky cities of the South and West,

or, indeed, to that vaster and more ancient city, whose streets are shadowless and voiceless, and whose gates are guarded by God.

But the mighty blind sea will ever chant the same mysterious hymn, under the same infinite light of blue, for those who shall come after them. . . .

V

. . . No electric nerves have yet penetrated this little world, to connect its humble life with the industrial and commercial activities of the continent: here the feverish speculator feels no security: — it is a fit sojourn for those only who wish to forget the harsh realities of city existence, the burning excitement of loss and gain, the stern anxieties of duty, — who care only to enjoy the rejuvenating sea, to drink the elixir of the perfect air, to dream away the long and luminous hours, perfumed with sweet, faint odors of summer. The little mail-boat, indeed, comes at regular intervals of days, and the majesty of the United States is represented by a post-office, — but the existence of that office could never be divined by the naked eye.

THE POST-OFFICE

A negro, who seemed to understand Spanish only, responded to my inquiries by removing a pipe from his lips, and pointing the cane-stem thereof toward a building that made a dark red stain against the green distance — with the words: *"Casa de correo? — si, señor! directamente detras del campo, señor; — sigue el camino carretero à la casa colorada."*

So I crossed plains thickly grown with a sturdy green weed bearing small yellow flowers, and traversed plank-bridges laid over creeks in which I saw cats fishing and swimming — actually swimming, for even the feline race loses its dread of water here; — and I followed a curving roadway half obliterated by wire-grass — until I found myself at last within a small farmyard, where cords of wood were piled up about an antique, gabled, chocolate-colored building that stood in the midst. I walked half around it, seeking for the entrance, — hearing only the sound of children's voices, and a baby's laughter; and finally came in front of an open gallery on the southern side, where a group of Creole children were, — two pretty blond infants, with an elder and darker sister. Seated in a rocking-chair, her infant brother sprawling at her feet, she was dancing a baby sister on her knee, chanting the while this extraordinary refrain: —

"*Zanimaux caquêne so maniê galoupé;* — *bourique,* — *tiquiti, tiquiti, tiquiti; milet,* — *tocolo, tocolo, tocolo; çouval,* — *tacata, tacata, tacata.*"

And with the regular *crescendo* of the three onomatopes, the baby went higher and higher. . . . My steps had made no sound upon the soft grass; the singer's back, inundated with chestnut hair, was turned toward me; but the baby had observed my approach, and its blue stare of wonder caused the girl to look round. At once she laid the child upon the floor, arose, and descended the wooden step to meet me with the question, — "Want to see papa?"

She might perhaps have been twelve, not older, — slight, with one of those sensitive, oval faces that reveal a Latin origin, and the pinkness of rich health bursting through its olive skin; — the eyes that questioned my face were brown and beautiful as a wild deer's.

"I want to get some stamped envelopes," I responded; — "is this the post-office?"

"Yes, sir; I can give them to you," she an-

swered, turning back toward the gallery steps;
— "come this way!"

I followed her as far as the doorway of the
tiniest room I had ever seen, — just large
enough to contain a safe, an office desk, and a
chair. It was cozy, carpeted, and well lighted
by a little window fronting the sea. I saw a
portrait hanging above the desk, — a singularly fine gray head, with prophetic features
and Mosaic beard, — the portrait of the island's patriarch. . . .

"You see," she observed, in response to my
amused gaze, while she carefully unlocked the
safe, — "when papa and mamma are at work
in the field, I have to take charge. Papa tells
me what to do. — How many did you say? —
four! — that will be ten cents. — Now, if you
have a letter to post, you can leave it here —
if you like."

I handed her my letter — a thick one —
in a two-cent envelope. She weighed it in her
slender brown hand; — I suspected the postage
was insufficient.

"It is too heavy," she said; — "you will
have to put another stamp on it, I think."

"In that case," I replied, "take back one of

the stamped envelopes, and give me instead a
two-cent stamp for my letter."

She hesitated a moment, with a pretty look
of seriousness, — and then answered: —

"Why, yes, I could do that; but — but that
would n't be doing fair by you" — passing
her fine thin fingers through the brown curls
in a puzzled way; — "no, that would n't be
fair to you."

"Of course it's fair," I averred encouragingly
— "we can't bother with fractions, and I have
no more small change. That is all right."

"No, it is n't all right," she returned, —
making the exchange with some reluctance; —
"it is n't right to take more than the worth
of our money; but I don't really know how to
fix it. I 'll ask papa when he comes home, and
we 'll send you the difference — if there is any.
— Oh! yes, I will! — I 'll send it to the hotel. —
It would n't be right to keep it."

All vain my protests.

"No, no! I 'm sure we owe you something.
Valentine! Léonie! — say good-bye, — nicely!"

So the golden-haired babies cooed their
"goo'bye," as I turned the corner, and waved
them kisses; — and as I reached the wagon-

road by the open gate, I heard again the bird-voice of the little post-mistress singing her onomatopoetic baby-song, *"Bourique, — tiquiti, tiquiti, tiquiti; milet, — tocoto, tocoto, tocoto; çouval, — tacata, tacata, tacata."*

VI

... O little brown-eyed lamb, the wolfish world waits hungrily to devour such as thou! — O dainty sea-land flower, that pinkness of thine will not fade out more speedily than shall evaporate thy perfume of sweet illusions in the stagnant air of cities! Many tears will dim those dark eyes, nevertheless, ere thou shalt learn that wealth — even the wealth of nations — is accumulated, without sense of altruism, in eternal violation of those exquisite ethics which seem to thee of God's own teaching. When thou shalt have learned this, and other and sadder things, perhaps, memory may crown thee with her crown of sorrows, — may bear thee back, back, in wonderful haze of blue and gold, to that island home of thine, — even into that tiny office-room, with its smiling gray portrait of thy dead father's father. And fancy may often re-create for thee

the welcome sound of hoofs returning home: —
"*çouval,* — *tacata, tacata, tacata.*" . . .

And dreaming of the funny little refrain, the
stranger fancied he could look into the future
of many years. . . . And in the public car of a
city railroad, he saw a brown-eyed, sweet-faced
woman, whom it seemed he had known a child,
but now with a child of her own — asleep there
in her arms — and so pale! It was sundown;
and her face was turned to the west, where lingered splendid mockeries of summer seas, —
golden Pacifics speckled with archipelagoes of
rose and fairy-green. But he knew in some
mysterious way that she was thinking of seas
not of mist, — of islands not of cloud, while the
heavy vehicle rumbled on its dusty way, and
the hoofs of the mule seemed to beat time to
an old Creole refrain — *Milet,* — *tocoto, tocoto
tocoto.*

THE END